Penguin Books
Lost Profile

Françoise Sagan was born in 1935. Her father is a prosperous Paris industrialist whose family were originally Spanish. She took her *nom de plume* from the Princesse de Sagan of Marcel Proust. She was eighteen years old when she wrote her best-selling *Bonjour Tristesse*. She had failed to pass her examinations at the Sorbonne and she decided to write a novel. The book received great acclaim in France, where in 1959 it sold 850,000 copies, and also abroad. Her second and third books, *A Certain Smile* and *Those Without Shadows*, have also had tremendous popularity in France, Great Britain and the U.S.A. These were followed by *Aimez-vous Brahms . . .* (1959), *Wonderful Clouds* (1961), *La Chamade* (1965), *The Heart-Keeper* (1968), *Sunlight on Cold Water* (1971), *Scars on the Soul* (1972), *Silken Eyes* (short stories, 1975) and *The Unmade Bed* (1977).

Françoise Sagan

Lost Profile

Translated from the French
by Joanna Kilmartin

Penguin Books

Penguin Books Ltd, Harmondsworth,
Middlesex, England
Penguin Books, 625 Madison Avenue,
New York, New York 10022, U.S.A.
Penguin Books Australia Ltd, Ringwood,
Victoria, Australia
Penguin Books Canada Ltd, 2801 John Street,
Markham, Ontario, Canada L3R 1B4
Penguin Books (N.Z.) Ltd, 182–190 Wairau Road,
Auckland 10, New Zealand

Un Profil perdu first published by Flammarion 1974
This translation first published by André Deutsch Limited 1976
Published in Penguin Books 1978

Made and printed in Great Britain by
Richard Clay (The Chaucer Press) Ltd,
Bungay, Suffolk
Set in Monotype Baskerville

To Peggy Roche

Mais ne suffit-il pas que tu sois l'apparence
Pour réjouir un cœur qui fuit la vérité?

CHARLES BAUDELAIRE

The party was at the Alferns' – a fashionable doctor with a rich wife – and I had been very reluctant to go. The kind of afternoon I'd just been through with Alan, my husband, an afternoon that had finally put paid to four years of love, violence, tenderness and revulsion, was one that I would have preferred to round off in the arms of Morpheus or Bacchus. At any rate, alone. But of course, supreme masochist that he was, Alan had insisted that we go to this party. He was his handsome self again, smiling when asked what the most devoted couple in Paris had been doing with themselves, and making some easy joking reply while keeping a tight grip on my elbow. I could see the two of us in the mirrors, and I too smiled at the charming picture we made: equally tall and slim, he blond and blue-eyed, I black-haired and grey-eyed, with the same gestures and, already apparent, the same air of profound defeat. Only he went a bit too far and when, in reply to some asinine female's tender inquiry 'When am I to be a god-mother, Alan?' he said that one man like him in my life was more than enough and that I didn't deserve two, I saw red. 'That's true,' I said, and as sometimes in a piece of music a sudden paroxysm announces the next theme, I shook off Alan's hand and turned my back on him. That was how, at a cocktail party indistinguishable from any other, in Paris in winter, I found myself face to face with Julius A. Cram. I had wrenched myself free so violently that I could feel Alan's back tremble with rage against my own. Julius

A. Cram – that was how he instantly introduced himself to me: Julius A. Cram – had a pale, colourless, inscrutable face. I asked him casually if he liked the pictures on show there: for the party was in fact a private view to launch the paintings of our exuberant hostess's lover.

'What's all this about pictures?' said Julius A. Cram. 'Ah, yes! I do believe I see one by the window.'

He made a sign, and instinctively I followed this little man upon whose cranium, since I was half a head taller, I could see the unmistakable signs of incipient baldness. He stopped abruptly in front of a canvas that looked as though it had been painted by someone who would have liked to be a painter, and stared up at it. His eyes were blue and round behind his spectacles and his eyelashes were in startling contrast to them: like a pirate's sails on a fishing boat. His contemplation lasted a full minute, then he uttered a harsh sound, closer to a dog's bark than human speech, in which I made out the word 'Ghastly!'. 'What?' I said, taken aback, for his bark seemed to me justified but exaggerated, and he repeated just as loudly, 'Ghastly!'. Our immediate neighbours fell back as though confronted by some outrage and I found myself alone, trapped between the picture and the fearless Julius A. Cram, apparently little disposed to allow me to escape. A low murmur arose behind us. Yes, Julius A. Cram had quite distinctly called that picture ghastly not once but twice, and the charming Josée Ash (i.e. me) hadn't raised the slightest protest. This murmur penetrated the sixth sense of the imposing Mme Debout, who turned towards us. Mme Debout was a person to be reckoned with. She ruled over this fashionable set with uncontested authority. At sixty plus, she was very slim, very dark, very elegant, and the fortune left her by her husband (long since dead of exhaustion) permitted her an exceptional degree of independence and severity. Whatever the circumstances, the marital dramas, the gala even-

8

ings, Mme Debout usually settled everything, occasionally ruined everything, and had always ended up alone, upright, as her name implied. Her likes and her dislikes were equally inflexible. She detected at once what was outdated in an avant-garde work and what was daring in a conventional one. Had it not been for this innate and unshakable perversity, she would have been intelligent.

Sensing that something untoward was going on, she made her way towards us, followed by her invisible retinue of men-at-arms, jesters and lackeys, for although she always went about alone, she seemed to be constantly surrounded by a menacing bodyguard. And this created around her a sort of forbidden zone that was almost tangible and that discouraged all familiarity.

'What were you saying, Julius?' she asked.

'I was just pointing out,' said Julius without flinching, 'that this picture is frightful.'

'Was that absolutely necessary?' she said. 'After all, it isn't as bad as all that.'

She waved a hand at the Saint Sebastian pierced with arrows so summarily dismissed by Julius. The tilt of her chin and the tone of her voice were perfect: a mixture of contempt for the work, pitying tolerance of our hostess's excesses, and a mild rebuke to Julius for his bad manners.

'The picture made me laugh,' said Julius A. Cram in a completely new, rather sibilant voice, 'I can't help that.'

Pamela Alfern, with Alan in tow, arrived on the scene, a look of inquiry on her face. She had heard some snapping, noticed a certain embarrassment among her guests, and came sailing into battle under full canvas.

'How do you like Cristobal's painting, Julius?' she said.

Without replying, Julius turned his fierce gaze on her. She recoiled slightly, then instantly recovered her hostess's poise.

'Have you met Alan Ash, Josée's husband?'

'Your husband?' Julius said.

I nodded. He began to laugh, a barbaric, primitive, repellent laugh that could truthfully be described as ghastly.

'What's so funny?' said Alan. 'Is it the picture that makes you laugh, or the fact that I'm married to Josée?'

Julius A. Cram glared at him. I was beginning to find him more and more outrageous. Whatever else, he didn't lack courage: to defy Mme Debout, his hostess and Alan all within the space of three minutes implied quite a nerve.

'I was laughing to myself, for no particular reason,' he said shortly. 'I fail to understand, my dear' – he was addressing Mme Debout – 'you're always complaining that I never laugh. Well, now you should be satisfied: I'm laughing.'

I suddenly remembered having heard about him. Julius A. Cram was a powerful business tycoon who wielded considerable political influence and probably knew all about the Swiss bank accounts of three-quarters of the guests. He was said to be generous and very tough; people were scared of him and invited him to everything. This explained the equivocal smiles, indulgent and forced at the same time, of Mme Debout and Pamela Alfern. We stood there, the four of us, looking at one another and finding nothing to say. Of course, all that Alan and I had to do was to take our leave, congratulate the artist who was parading about in the hall, and return to our own private hell. But it seemed as though this situation, so easily resolved, after all, with a few words such as 'Good-bye, see you again soon' or 'So nice to have met you', was beyond recall. It was retrieved by Julius who clearly saw himself as tribal organizer-in-chief and who suggested to me that we should go and have a drink at the bar at the other end of the room. Once again, and with the same gesture, he took charge of me and we were across the room in no time. I was midway between laughter and apprehension, for Alan's face had gone noticeably pale and his eyes almost glassy with anger. I gulped down the glass of vodka that Julius A. Cram without consulting me had thrust imperiously into my hand. The buzz of party conversation had resumed around us and, after a moment or two, I felt that for once a scene had been avoided.

'Let's be serious,' said Julius A. Cram. 'What do you do in life?'

'Nothing,' I answered with a hint of pride.

And it's true that in the midst of all these idlers who never stopped talking about their little creative efforts – interior design, Finnish-style jewellery, ceramics, and other ventures of one kind or another – I was happy to acknowledge my own total idleness. I was Alan's wife, and he supported me. And suddenly I knew that I was going to leave him and that I could no longer accept anything from him, ever again, not a single dollar or a single contact. I was going to have to work, to join the happy band of vague press officers, PROs, and the like. And I should be lucky if I managed to break into that privileged circle where one could stay in bed until nine and get away to the sun two or three times a year. There had always been someone, first my parents, then Alan, between me and material cares. This happy time now seemed to be at an end and I, poor fool, felt as pleased as if I were about to embark on some sort of adventure.

'And you like doing nothing?'

Julius A. Cram looked at me without disapproval. He seemed amiably intrigued.

'Certainly,' I said. 'I watch the time pass, the days go by, I lie in the sun, when there is any, I don't know what I shall be doing from one day to the next. And if I suddenly develop a passion for something, I have time to devote myself to it. Everyone ought to be able to do the same.'

'Perhaps,' he said pensively. 'I've never thought about it.

I've worked all my life . . . but that's what I like doing,' he added in an apologetic tone that I found endearing.

He was a strange man, vulnerable and menacing at the same time. There was something struggling inside him, something unrelenting and desperate that was perhaps responsible for that barking laugh. Oh no, I thought to myself, I'm not going to start getting involved in the psychology of businessmen, in their success and their loneliness. When people are very rich and very lonely, they've usually asked for it.

'Your husband never stops looking at you,' he said. 'What have you done to him?'

Why did he automatically cast me as the villain? And what was I to say to him? That I had loved my husband, hadn't loved him enough, had loved him too much, or for the wrong reasons? Even supposing I wanted to, what could I tell him that would represent the truth? A truth with which Alan himself would agree . . .

That, surely, is the worst thing about a break-up: not just leaving one another, but leaving one another for different reasons. After having been so happy, so involved with one another, so close that nothing is real except through one another's eyes, you both wind up lost, frantic, searching the desert for paths that will never cross again.

'It's getting late,' I said. 'I must go.'

At which point Julius A. Cram, in a solemn but self-satisfied tone of voice, began to sing the praises of a tea room called the Salina and invited me to meet him there two days later at five o'clock, unless of course I thought the idea too old-fashioned. I agreed, a bit taken aback, and left him; then I made my way towards Alan, towards a night of recriminations, blows, tears, probably for the last time, while echoing in my head was the phrase 'They have the best *profiteroles* in Paris.'

Such was my first encounter with Julius A. Cram.

'A rum baba,' I said.

I was sitting at a table in the Salina Tea Rooms, distraught and out of breath. It was not so much a rum baba that I needed as a real rum, the condemned man's tot. For the last two days I had been riddled by all the guns of love, jealousy, despair. Alan's entire arsenal trained on me yet again and firing at point-blank range; for two whole days he had not allowed me to leave the flat and it was a miracle that I had remembered this eccentric rendezvous with Julius A. Cram in a tea room.

Had I been meeting a friend, someone I was really close to, I would have been tempted to confide in him – something I loathed. I dreaded those all too common confessions in which the women of my generation seemed to delight. I never knew how to explain myself and was always afraid of being persuaded that I was in the wrong. Besides, in this case there were only two alternatives: the first was to put up with Alan and our shared life and the fact that we continually found ourselves face down in the dirt, hearts battered, minds adrift; the second was to leave, get away from him, escape. But there were times when I no longer knew what to do: I would remember him as he was when I loved him and then I lost all sense of myself, as well as of the power to make that decision which I knew to be the only rational one.

At first, in this tea room where hungry young people and twittering old ladies fluttered in unison, I had a sense of well-being, of security: guarded by generations of un-compromisingly English puddings and fulminating French *éclairs* oblivious to everything – including me. I felt like smiling, enjoying life again. I looked at Julius A. Cram for the first time. He seemed very respectable, very gentle, a bit crumpled. One felt that after a couple of days his beard would not so much break out over his skin as prick its way through on the sly. I forgot his business deals, the savage energy he deployed in order to bring them off, I forgot, thanks to that adolescent characteristic, Cram's famed and brutal power. Instead of an industrial magnate I saw an elderly baby. My senses often play me false. But almost as often they indulge me, which is why I bear them no grudge.

'Two teas, one rum baba, one *frangipane*,' said Julius.

'At once, Monsieur Cram,' intoned the waitress, and, after executing a strange sort of pirouette, she disappeared down a corridor of screens.

I watched her with the exaggerated attentiveness one instinctively accords to everyone and everything after a near fatal accident. 'I'm in a tea room with a tycoon, and we've ordered a *frangipane* and a rum baba,' whispered my memory, while my heart and my mind could see only Alan's handsome face, ugly with rage, peering over the banisters. I knew plenty of bars and restaurants and night clubs in various corners of our fair planet. Tea rooms were unknown territory (this one, it seemed to me, even more so than most) and the atmosphere of *toile de Jouy* and curtseys, white aprons and starched caps, gave me an almost unbearable sense of false security. It was no use: it was definitely more in my line to sob with rage and misery on the carpet, my hair all over the place, in front of an equally tormented man of my own age, than to nibble pastries with a well-behaved stranger. One some-times has such moments of insight, just like that, purely 'visual', but ineradicable. The rest of the time you drift along without seeing yourself, you let yourself sink in a trail of brackish, colourless bubbles down to the lowest depths, blind, deaf and dumb with despair. Or else you re-emerge glorious and triumphant in someone else's eyes, blinded by the sun that you represent for him and that he invents at his heart's peril. Needless to say, of course, I didn't go into all that there and then – as a matter of fact I never talked to myself, having always found other people more interesting, more absorbing. I merely wondered to myself whether *frangipane* was yellow or coffee-coloured. No doubt somewhere between the two. In the end, not knowing what to say to him, I put the question to Julius. He seemed extremely bored, shrugged his shoulders – a clear sign of ignorance in a man – and asked me how Alan was. I replied briefly that he was well.

'And you?'

'Me too, of course.'

'Of course . . . that's no answer.'

He was beginning to irritate me. It may not have been an answer but it was the only one I could give. Unless I were to give him a detailed account of my childhood, my various love affairs and my tormented marriage to Alan, there was nothing I could tell him. After all, I didn't know him. And I saw him neither as friend nor confidant. That *frangipane* seemed to be an age in coming.

'I'm being tactless,' he said in a decisive, almost triumphant tone of voice.

I made a vague gesture of denial, looked at my trembling hands and searched for my cigarettes in the bottom of my bag.

'I've always been tactless,' Julius A. Cram went on. 'Or rather,' he added, 'I tend to go about things the wrong way. I want to know everything about you. I know I ought to begin by talking to you about the weather, but I don't seem to be able to.'

I asked myself silently how talking about the weather would have made things any better. Suddenly he seemed to me not only tactless but crude and lacking in charm. If he didn't possess the tiny glimmer of imagination needed to make small talk, above all small talk, he should have known better than to invite me to this ridiculous tea room. I wanted to get up and go, to leave him there alone with his pastries, and only the fear of what awaited me outside, of breaking down in the street and then beating a hasty retreat to that dreadful flat, prevented me.

'Come on, he's a human being,' I told myself, 'we must have something to say to one another. It isn't natural . . .' And indeed it was certainly the first time I had experienced this sensation of constraint and stiffness in someone's company, this longing to escape. Naturally I attributed it to the state of my nerves, to the sleeplessness of the past few nights, to my lack of poise; in fact I did exactly what I shouldn't have done: I blamed myself rather than Julius for the awkwardness of those first few minutes. All my life, it seemed, a sort of guilty conscience, amounting almost to feeblemindedness, had led me to shoulder this kind of vague responsibility. I had arrived feeling guilty about Alan. Now I felt guilty about Julius A. Cram, and it was a safe bet that if the sprightly waitress were to go sprawling on the carpet with the *frangipane*, I would think it was my fault. A feeling of anger against myself and the hopeless mess I was making of my life began to take possession of me.

'And you,' I said in a controlled voice, 'what do you do?'

'Business deals,' replied Julius A. Cram. 'To be exact, I've done a lot of business deals. Nowadays, I spend my time checking up on them. I live in a car that takes me from one office to another. I check up and then I move on again.'

'What fun,' I said. 'And apart from that? Are you married?'

16

For a moment he seemed taken aback, as though I had said something shocking. Perhaps I was supposed to know he was a bachelor.

'No,' he said, 'I'm not married, but I nearly was.'

He made this pronouncement in so pompous and solemn a tone that I looked at him askance.

'Didn't it work out?' I asked.

'We weren't from the same background.'

The tea room seemed to freeze before my eyes. What on earth was I doing there, sitting opposite this snobbish businessman?

'She was an aristocrat,' said Julius A. Cram ruefully. 'An English aristocrat.'

For the second time I stared at him in amazement. If this man didn't interest me, he certainly surprised me.

'And in what way did the fact that she was an aristocrat . . .'

'I'm a self-made man,' said Julius A. Cram, 'and when I met her, I was still very young and ill at ease socially.'

'Whereas now,' I said intrigued, 'you feel quite at ease?'

'Oh now, yes,' he said. 'You see, the point about money, perhaps the only point, is that one feels at ease everywhere.'

And as though to underline this outrageous statement, he tapped his teaspoon against his cup.

'She lived in Reading,' he went on dreamily. 'Do you know Reading? It's a little town near London. I met her on a picnic. Her father was a colonel.'

Obviously, if I wanted to be taken out of myself, I'd have done better to have gone straight to a cinema and buried myself in one of those orgies of sex and violence that were so popular at the time. This picnic in Reading with a colonel's daughter wasn't exactly calculated to kindle the imagination of a young woman at her wits' end. It was just my luck. For once I meet a really high-powered tycoon, and I instantly hit upon his weak point, the chink in his armour: an English fiancée who is too upper-class. I found it easier to imagine Julius A. Cram driving a dozen New York bankers to suicide. I took the precaution of tasting my rum baba with the tip of my tongue – I've always loathed pastries. Julius A. Cram must still have been walking the green hills of Berkshire in his thoughts. He was silent.

'And since then?'

Having got this far, common politeness demanded that I at least finish my cup of tea.

'Oh, since then, nothing much,' said Julius A. Cram, and blushed. 'A few escapades, perhaps.'

For a moment I imagined him in a specialist brothel, surrounded by naked girls. My head swam. It was unthinkable. Any idea of sexuality was incompatible with Julius A. Cram's looks, his voice, his complexion. I wondered where he found his strength in this imperfect world given his apparent lack of the two principal motivating forces of human beings in general: vanity and sexuality. I realized that I didn't understand the man at all. In the ordinary way, this realization would have excited my curiosity but instead it left me disconcerted and rather uneasy. I seem to remember that we did talk about the weather after all and that I agreed with feigned enthusiasm to meet him again the following week in the same place at the same time. To tell the truth, I would have agreed to anything in order to extricate myself.

I walked home slowly, and it wasn't until I was crossing the Pont Royal that I was suddenly overcome with laughter. The occasion had not only been preposterous, it had been literally indescribable. And yet, perhaps because of its very absurdity, I retained a rather pleasant memory of it in the days that followed.

A fortnight later, I had completely forgotten this interlude. I had telephoned Julius A. Cram, or rather his secretary, to cancel our appointment, and the following day I had received an enormous bouquet and a card expressing his deep disappointment. For a few days, before wilting and dying where it lay, this sheaf of flowers had been a bright, cheerful and somewhat incongruous presence in a flat which had become bleak, functional, desert-like, as though laid waste by the inferno which Alan and I so assiduously created there.

The situation had stabilized, if that's the word. Alan no longer left the flat. If I wanted to go out, he followed me. If the telephone rang, which happened less and less frequently, he picked up the receiver, said 'There's no one here' and hung up. The rest of the time he walked round the flat like a madman, nursing his grievances, inventing new ones, interrogating me, waking me up whenever I went to sleep, one moment crying like a child over the death of our love, wailing that it was all his fault, the next reproaching me bitterly and with ever-increasing violence. It seemed to me that this vortex, this abyss into which we were sinking a little further each day must have a limit, and that there was nothing for it but to wait. I bathed, I cleaned my teeth, I dressed and undressed in response to God knows what reflex dating from my previous existence. The maid, appalled, had left us a week before. We ate out of tins, separately, and I found myself wrestling clumsily

with tins of sardines that I didn't want but that I knew
I must eat. The flat was like a rudderless boat whose skipper,
Alan, had gone mad. And I, the sole passenger, had lost
all trace, for ever, of a sense of humour. As for our friends,
some of whom telephoned while others, more persistent,
knocked at the door (to be instantaneously ejected by Alan),
I doubt if they had the least idea of what was going on
between those four walls. They may even have thought we
were in the middle of a second honeymoon.

In this whirlwind of threats, entreaties, regrets, promises,
half beaten, half raped, I lived outside myself, terror stricken.
Twice I attempted to escape, but Alan caught up with me
on the stairs and forced me back, step by step, once without
saying a word, once muttering intolerable obscenities in
English. We were completely cut off from the outside world.
Alan had broken the radio, then the television set, and I
suspect he only refrained from cutting the telephone wires
for the pleasure of seeing me start up in hope, a very tenu-
ous hope, whenever it happened to ring. I would take
sleeping pills the moment I felt the tears coming, whatever
the time of day or night, and thus, falling into a nightmare-
ridden sleep, I would escape him for four hours, four
hours during which he would shake me incessantly and call
my name aloud or in a whisper, putting his ear to my heart
to make sure I was still alive and that his beloved had not
escaped him, through a final ruse, by taking a few pills too
many. Once and only once, I cracked. Through the window
I saw an open car go by with a young couple in it laughing
together, and it seemed to me like an extra slap in the face –
from fate, this time – a reminder of what I had been, of
what I might have been, of what, in my bewilderment, I
felt I had lost for ever. That was the day I began to weep.
I implored Alan to go or to let me go. I pleaded with him
in childish phrases such as 'please' and 'I beg of you'

and 'do be kind' that were ludicrously inappropriate. And he would be there beside me, stroking my hair, consoling me, begging me to stop crying, saying that my tears were too much for him to bear. During those two or three hours, he became his old self, tender, trusting, protective. I swear that he felt comforted, and suffered less. For myself, I can't say that I suffered much. It was both worse and less serious at the same time. I was waiting for Alan either to go away or to kill me. Not for a moment did it occur to me to kill myself: there was an ineradicable, inaccessible being inside me – the person who caused Alan so much misery, the same person who was waiting. Nevertheless there were times when the waiting seemed illusory, pointless, and then I was overcome with a paroxysm of despair, I literally shook all over, my muscles knotted, my throat went dry, and I was incapable of moving.

One afternoon at about three o'clock, I was wandering about the study looking for a book that I had started the day before and that Alan, typically, must have hidden since he couldn't bear anything to distract me, even momentarily, from him, from what he called 'us'. He hadn't yet snatched a book from my hands, some remnant of good manners no doubt restraining him, just as he still stood aside in doorways to let me pass and lit my cigarettes. Anyway he had hidden this book, and as I got down on the floor to look for it under the sofa, I knew that if he came into the room he would start laughing, but I was quite beyond caring.

It was then that the doorbell rang for the first time in four days, and I got to my feet and listened for the sharp click as Alan shut the door in the face of some importunate caller. After a minute or two I heard Alan's voice, calm and ingratiating, and, intrigued, I went out into the hall. There in the hall, actually inside the hall, that is having crossed the threshold, stood Julius A. Cram, hat in hand. I was thunderstruck. How had he managed to get so far? He saw me, walked towards me just as though Alan were not blocking his path, and Alan stepped back involuntarily. Julius held out his hand. I stared at him. The casting was all wrong: it might have been the police, the fire brigade, Parsifal, Alan's mother, anyone but him.

'How are you?' he said. 'I was telling your husband that we'd arranged to meet at the Salina today, and that I'd taken the liberty of coming to pick you up.'

I didn't reply but stood looking at Alan who appeared transfixed with amazement and fury. As Julius turned towards him I saw once again that look of his that had struck me for the first time at the Alferns', a look of icy ferocity, the look of a predator. It was a strange scene: I saw a young, unshaven man beside an open door, I saw a grim-looking middle-aged man in a navy blue overcoat, and I saw myself, a dishevelled young woman in a dressing gown, leaning against another door. I couldn't tell which of the three was the intruder.

'My wife is unwell,' Alan said curtly. 'There's no question of her going out.'

Julius's eyes, fierce as ever, turned back to me, and in a loud, peremptory voice he barked out some words that sounded much more like an order than an invitation:

'I'm expecting her to join me for tea. I'll go and sit in the drawing room,' he added for my benefit, 'it won't take you long to get dressed.'

Alan took a step towards him, very quickly, but already someone had appeared in the doorway; in the massive shape of Julius's chauffeur the fourth character in this second-rate farce entered the flat. He too was dressed in navy blue and held his gloves in his hand, and he too had that same vague, neutral air that made them both look as I imagined Gestapo agents would look.

'There was something I wanted to ask you,' Julius said, turning to Alan. 'Am I right in thinking that this flat faces north-east?'

Then all of a sudden something clicked inside me, shook me out of my paralysis, shattered the impression of unreality, and I rushed into my room, locked the door, grabbed a pair of trousers and a sweater and hurriedly pulled them on. I could hear my teeth chattering and my heart thumping in my haste. Then I picked up a couple of shoes that looked as though they might be a pair, unlocked the door and made a dash for the drawing room and Julius A. Cram. I hadn't taken more than a minute or so, I was pouring with sweat, and only some remnant of self-respect prevented me from flinging myself at the chauffeur, grabbing his arm and telling him to get going, put his foot down and drive as far away as possible. As it was, I backed down the corridor and out of the door, keeping Julius between me and Alan, and before Julius himself closed the door I caught a glimpse of Alan against the light, his arms dangling and his mouth set in a sort of hideous grin. He looked horrifyingly like a real madman.

The car was an old Daimler, long and broad as a lorry, and I suddenly remembered having seen it outside the block of flats for days on end during my rare excursions as far as the window.

To judge from the sun, we were driving west. But I no longer believed even in the sun. Lost in the desert of that enormous car and of my impoverished heart, I tried idiotically to identify north, south, east and west. In vain. Perhaps the slanting shadows that fell across the bonnet of the car, on one of those motorways punctuated with monotonous hoardings and blank-looking houses, no longer meant anything. But eventually we went through Mantes-la-Jolie, and having turned into a lane, arrived at a semi-fortified manor. Julius had said nothing. He hadn't even patted my hand. In any case, he wasn't a demonstrative man. He climbed in and out of his car, lit his cigarettes, put on his overcoat, neutrally, without either clumsiness or grace. And as I'd always been drawn to people because of their gestures, the way they moved or didn't move, it was like sitting next to a dummy or an invalid. I had shivered throughout the journey, at first out of terror lest Alan should follow us, suddenly appear at a traffic light and jump on to the bonnet, or materialize as a traffic cop and halt for ever my flight towards what was no doubt a derisory freedom, but freedom nonetheless. Then, when the motorway began and sheer speed made such highway robbery impossible, I had shivered with loneliness.

I was alone, deprived of Alan's continuous, inescapable and by now to me almost incestuous proximity. Now it was back to 'I, me, myself', instead of 'we', horrifying though that 'we' had become. Where had the other gone? The other – executioner or victim, it made no difference – at all events the partner in the reckless, pernicious but irresistible ragtimes of the past years. Fundamentally, in my own eyes, I saw myself as a girl left standing on the dance floor, her partner snatched away forever by some unforeseen circumstance, rather than as a wife deprived of her husband. And how we had danced, Alan and I, to every conceivable rhythm and between countless sheets. Swooning and assuaged, we had shared the tender truces of passion and only his jealousy, against which he was helpless, had made our relationship impossible. Sick though he was, he alone, in the end, had remained to heap the sticks of memory, imagination and suffering on to the funeral pyre of our love. That was why I had let it go on for so long, and why, on the motorway, I felt obscurely guilty: guilty of not having loved him for longer, guilty of indifference, a word that horrified me. I knew that indifference was the joker, the ace of trumps, in every emotional relationship, and I despised it. Wild passion I admired, and loyalty and spontaneity and even a certain kind of fidelity. It had taken a good few years of casualness and cynicism for me to reach that point, but I had reached it nonetheless, and if I hadn't had an instinctive, animal loathing for what is called the pleasure of pain, I should certainly have stayed with Alan.

Julius A. Cram's fortified manor or castle was a model of its kind. Built in the shape of a horseshoe of massive stone, it had loophole windows and drawbridge doors and Louis XIII furniture that, in view of Julius's wealth, was probably genuine. Stags' heads gave the entrance hall a funereal aspect, and a stone staircase with a wrought-iron banister led to the upper floors. As a concession to the twentieth century the manservant wore a white jacket, but I should have preferred him in a jerkin. He looked for my suitcase, and naturally failing to find it, withdrew. Julius, having asked me at least five times if I was all right without waiting for a reply, led the way into the drawing room. It had everything: leather sofas, shelves full of books, animal skins, and an immense fireplace in which someone had just lit a huge fire. Yes, on second thoughts, there was something missing: a dog. I asked Julius whether he had a dog and he answered yes, of course, but they were in the kennels, where you'd expect dogs to be, and as it was getting dark he would show them to me in the morning. He had beagles, labradors, terriers, etcetera.

It would be untrue to say, since I replied to his questions, that I didn't hear what he said. It was simply that the person who listened to him and answered him was not me. At least, not the person I felt myself to be. The manservant reappeared with the drinks tray, and I fell upon a glass of vodka and drained it at a gulp. Julius seemed worried – he himself, he told me, had drunk nothing but tomato juice for nearly thirty years. An uncle of his had died of cirrhosis of the liver, and so had his grandfather, and it was a family disease he wished to avoid. I nodded; then, no doubt somewhat restored by my dose of Russian elixir, I asked him the question that was tormenting me.

'How did you come to turn up at my flat this afternoon?'

'When you didn't keep our appointment, our second appointment,' Julius began, 'I was very surprised . . .'

I slid deeper into the leather sofa, wondering what he had found so surprising about my defection. Perhaps it was a new experience for someone in his position to be stood up.

'I was rather surprised,' Julius went on, 'particularly as I had very warm memories of our meeting at the Salina.'

I nodded, marvelling yet again at the mysteries of non-communication.

'You see,' Julius continued, 'I never talk about myself to anyone, and that afternoon I told you something that no one else knows, except, of course, Harriet.'

I looked at him blankly. Who on earth was Harriet? Had I gone from one madman to another?

'The English girl,' explained Julius. 'That business has been a constant source of irritation to me. I was made to look rather a fool, I've never been able to talk about it, and suddenly, at the Salina, I saw something in your eyes that made me feel that you wouldn't laugh at me. I can't tell you how much good that did me. And you yourself seemed so relaxed, so trusting . . . I very much wanted to see you again.'

He made this statement slowly, rather hesitantly.

'But how did you manage to find me?' I said.

'I made inquiries. First I asked among your friends myself, then I sent my secretaries to interrogate your concierge, your daily woman, and so on. I hesitated a long time before interfering in your private life, but in the end I decided it was my duty. I knew perfectly well,' he added with a triumphant little smile, 'that only something serious could have prevented you from keeping our appointment on Wednesday the twelfth at the Salina.'

I was torn between laughter, helpless laughter, and fury, entirely justifiable fury. What right had this stranger to question my friends, my maid, the concierge? By what token had he dared to indulge his curiosity and his wealth at my expense? Was it really because I hadn't laughed in his face when he told me about his pathetic romance with an English colonel's daughter? It seemed inconceivable. There were more than enough people to fawn on him and put on a show of sympathy with his sad tale. He was lying to me, but why? He must have known and sensed that he didn't attract me, and had no hope of ever doing so. Such pacts of non-aggression or non-complicity are often formed between a man and a woman at the very first glance. Not even vanity is proof against this kind of almost canine instinct. For a moment I hated him, with his self-assurance and his Louis XIII furniture. I hated him intensely. I held out my glass without a word, and, tut-tutting reproachfully – did he expect his ancestors' cirrhosis to put me off alcohol for ever? – he went to pour me another drink.

So, here I was in a house to the west of Paris, a Louis XIII manor with an ultra-rich banker-detective for proprietor, without transport, without luggage and without object, without the slightest idea as to my future, immediate or distant – and moreover night had fallen. I had been in a good many bizarre, comic or sinister situations in my life, but this time I was beating all my own records in absurdity. I gave myself a tender thought, a sort of private pat on the back, and took a gulp from the glass of vodka that seemed to be my sole earthly possession. I soon realized that I couldn't have paid much attention to the quality, let alone the quantity, of my daily ration of tinned food, for my head was already beginning to swim. The idea of seeing Julius A. Cram in triplicate alarmed me.

'How about a record?' I said.

Now it was Julius's turn to be disconcerted: no doubt he expected a different reaction from a young woman rescued from a sadistic husband. He got up and went to open a cabinet which was needless to say a period piece but which concealed some superb stereophonic equipment – Japanese-made, he informed me. In view of the décor I was expecting some Vivaldi, but it was Tebaldi's voice that filled the room.

'Do you like opera?' Julius asked.

Squatting like that in front of a panel of nickel-plated knobs, he looked taller than he really was.

'I've got the whole of *Tosca*,' he went on in the same almost triumphant tone.

It occurred to me that this man was oddly proud of everything. Not only of his elaborate and indeed admirable stereo set, but equally of Tebaldi herself. Could it be that I was in the presence of the only rich man I had come across who got real pleasure out of his money? If this was true it implied great virtue on his part, for in my experience the really rich, on the pretext, reiterated *ad nauseam*, that money is a double-edged weapon, felt obliged to flay themselves with it unremittingly, knowing they were courted, envied, ostracized, all because of their wealth and yet quite unable to use it to obtain the slightest relief. If they were generous they felt they were being cheated, and if they were cautious they were continually, and in the saddest possible way, being confirmed in the justice of their attitude. But in the case of Julius A. Cram – was it perhaps the vodka? – I had the impression that if he was proud, it was not so much of his business ability as of what it enabled him to do – for instance to listen to the admirable voice of a woman he admired, the great Tebaldi, without the slightest hiss or scratch, absolutely intact and pure. Just as, more ingenuously, he must have been proud of his efficiency, or the efficiency of his secretaries, which had enabled him to deliver a charming young woman, to wit, me, from what he regarded as a hideous fate.

'When will you get a divorce?'

'Who told you I wanted a divorce,' I replied crossly.

'You can't stay with that man,' said Julius with a practical air, 'he's sick.'

'And how do you know I don't like sick people?'

At the same time I was annoyed at my own unfairness. In so far as I had fallen in with my rescuer, it was only reasonable that I should offer him a few explanations. It was just that I wanted to keep them short.

'Alan isn't sick,' I said, 'he's obsessed. He's the sort of boy ... of man,' I corrected myself, 'who's born madly jealous. I didn't realize it until it was too late, but I'm as much to blame as he is, in a way.'

'Really? In what way?' queried Julius in his nasal voice.

He was standing over me with one hand on his hip, in the aggressive stance adopted by courtroom lawyers in American films.

'In that I failed to reassure him,' I said. 'He always distrusted me, however wrongly. It must have been my fault to some extent.'

'He was simply afraid you'd leave him,' Julius said, 'and because he was afraid, it happened. It's only logical.'

Tebaldi was singing one of the great arias and the accompaniment that surged up behind her made me want to break something. And also to burst into tears. No doubt about it, I was short of sleep.

'You'll say it's none of my business,' Julius went on.

'Yes,' I said savagely, 'that's right, it's none of your business.'

He didn't seem in the least put out. He looked at me almost pityingly, as though I'd dropped a brick. He waved his hand in a gesture that implied 'She doesn't know what she's saying', and this was the last straw. I got to my feet and poured myself another large vodka. I decided to make myself clear.

'Monsieur Cram, I don't know you. I know nothing about you except that you're rich, that you nearly married an English girl, and that you like *frangipane*.'

He repeated the same eloquent, resigned gesture, as of a reasonable man confronted with an irrational female.

'I also know,' I continued, 'that for reasons which escape me, you took an interest in me, made inquiries about me and then arrived on the scene just in time to extricate me from an unpleasant situation, for which I'm extremely grateful. That's the beginning and end of our relationship.'

At which point I sat down again, exhausted, and glared into the fire. To tell the truth, I felt more like laughing, for during my brief speech Julius had slowly retreated and was now standing in a distinctly unflattering pose framed between two sets of antlers.

'You're overwrought,' he said perspicaciously.

'Exceedingly,' I replied, 'anyone would be in my place. Do you have any sleeping pills?'

He gave such a start that I burst out laughing. In fact, from the moment I arrived there I had been alternating non-stop between tears and laughter, anger and stupefaction, and I was beginning to long in earnest for a nice, comfortable bed, which would in all probability be Gothic, on which to rest my weary head. I felt as though I could sleep for three days.

'Don't worry,' I told Julius. 'I'm not thinking of committing suicide here or anywhere else. It's simply that, as your secretary must have told you, the last few days have been pretty rough and I don't want to talk about them.'

He winced at the word 'secretary'. He came and sat down opposite me, crossing his legs. And I automatically registered that he had big feet.

'Quite apart from my secretaries who are devoted to me, I also talked a great deal to your friends who are equally devoted to you. They were worried about you.'

'Well, you can reassure them,' I said sarcastically. 'I'm safe here, for a few days at least.'

We looked at each other defiantly, but the exact nature of the challenge escaped me. What was I doing there? What was he thinking? What did he want to know about me, and why? As in the Tea Rooms, my hands had begun to tremble again. I badly needed some sleep. A few more drinks, a few more questions and I should collapse in tears on the shoulder of this stranger, who, perhaps, was just waiting for that very thing to happen.

'Would you be kind enough to show me to my room,' I said, getting to my feet.

Flanked by Julius and his manservant, I climbed the stairs and found myself as expected in a Gothic bedroom. I bade them good night, opened the window, briefly inhaled the deliciously cool country air and jumped into bed. I scarcely had time to close my eyes.

Naturally, I awoke next morning in a very good mood: the room was no less gloomy, the situation no less confused, but something inside me whistled a jaunty little tune. I've always been somehow out of key. As if life were a grand piano on which I neglected to use the pedals, or rather used them wrongly: soft-pedalling the symphonic overtures of my happiness and my successes, and attacking loudly the moonlight sonatas of my sadness. Listless when I should have been rejoicing, gay in the face of misfortune, I had constantly confounded the expectations, not to say the feelings, of all those who loved me. Not out of perversity, but simply because life seemed to me so crude at times, so absurd in its over-simplifications, that something inside me longed to bang down the lid on it, brutally, as one sometimes wishes one could do to certain pianists. Only the pianist, or at any rate one of the pianists, was myself. Which of the two of us had come off worse? There was Alan, no doubt lying hunched up on a sofa with his hands over his eyes, hearing nothing but the beating of his heart, and thirty miles away there was me, stretched out comfortably and listening expectantly for the cry of a bird already heard once that night. But which of us was the more alone? Was a broken heart, however painful, any worse than an anonymous, echoless solitude? For a moment my thoughts returned to Julius and I began to laugh. If that man hoped to get me into his clutches, to place me on some pre-selected square on his well-organized businessman's chessboard, he was doomed to disappointment. The jaunty little tune resounded more gaily than ever. I was still young, I was free once more, I was attractive and the sun was shining. No one was going to lay hands on me again for a while. I would get dressed, have breakfast and go back to Paris to find some sort of job and friends who would welcome me with open arms.

The manservant entered the room, pushing a trolley laden with toast and flowers from the garden, and informed me that Monsieur Cram had had to go to Paris but would be home for luncheon, that is, within the hour. I must have slept for fourteen hours. I went downstairs, sporting my old sweater and my new-found egotism, and wandered into the courtyard. It was empty. There was no sign of life save the shadowy figures that could be seen flitting past the windows, and the atmosphere was one of vague expectancy, of people awaiting the master of the house, without any real animation. Julius A. Cram's existence was clearly not as much fun as all that. I went round to the kennels, stroked three dogs who licked my hands, and decided to get myself one as soon as I got back to Paris. I would feed him and cherish him, this dog, by the sweat of my brow and the warmth of my affection, and he wouldn't reward me later by biting my ankles and asking me questions. In fact, although the present situation was a great deal more complicated, I had exactly the same feeling as when I emerged from boarding-school fifteen or twenty years earlier, but this time I was aware of it. One always thinks that one's feelings, because of a change of partner, or life style or age group, are different from those of one's adolescence, whereas they are precisely the same. And yet, each time, the desire to be free, the desire to be loved, the instinct to escape, the instinct of the chase, all seem, thanks to a providential amnesia or a naïve presumptuousness, to be completely new and original.

On my way back to the house I ran into Mme Debout. I was so flabbergasted that I allowed myself to be hugged convulsively three times before blurting out rudely, 'What are you doing here?'

'Julius has told me everything,' exclaimed that arbitress of etiquette, that connoisseur of delicate situations. 'He spoke to me first thing this morning and here I am.'

She had tucked my arm beneath hers and as she stumbled over the gravel she kept patting me with her gloved hand. She was wearing an olive-green suede outfit which was extremely elegant but which did nothing for her town make-up in the pale sunlight.

'I've known Julius for twenty years,' she said, 'and he has always had a strong sense of the proprieties. He didn't want this business to look like a secret abduction, so he telephoned me.'

She was splendid in her *Three Musketeers* style. She must have taken my silence for gratitude and went on:

'It didn't inconvenience me in the least. I had a boring lunch at Lasserre and I was only too pleased to be able to do what I could for the pair of you. How does one get into this wretched place?' she added in a stentorian voice, for it really was rather cold for her olive-green suit. A door opened as if by magic to reveal the lugubrious manservant, and we entered the drawing room.

'How gloomy it is here,' she said, as she glanced round the room. 'One might be in Cornwall.'

'I've never been to Cornwall.'

'You've never been to stay with Broderick? Broderick Cranfield? No? Well, it's like this, a shooting lodge. Of course it's more authentic, being in the middle of the moors instead of thirty miles from Paris.'

With that she sat down and took stock of me. I looked peaky, she declared, and it was hardly surprising. She had always thought Alan extremely odd. As did everyone else

35

in Paris. And because she had been a friend of my parents, she had been very worried about me. Since I hadn't the faintest idea that she knew my parents, I listened to this flow of revelations with astonishment. And when she wound up by informing me that I was to go back to Paris with her, that she would lend me a little flat belonging to one of her step-daughters who was at present in the Argentine, I nodded docilely.

No question about it, Julius A. Cram hadn't yet finished surprising me. There seemed to be nothing that he didn't have up his sleeve: chauffeur-bodyguards, private detectives, devoted secretaries, aristocratic fiancées, and now a duenna. And what a duenna! A woman whose acts of ferocity were only equalled – in number – by her good works, a woman as odious as she was elegant, in other words one of those women who are said to be beyond reproach. Julius A. Cram must have been powerful indeed for her to have noticed my existence and deigned to intervene. After all, I was a mere nobody in her eyes. If she had known my parents it must have been before the war; I had spent my youth in quite a different social circle before going to live in America and coming back arm in arm with that elegant young man called Alan, about whom she knew nothing except that he was well-off, American and a little odd. That Julius should have been smitten with me was not very serious. She would decide later whether to make me one of her hangers-on or one of her victims.

Julius arrived punctually and seemed delighted to see his two women gossiping by the fire. He thanked Mme Debout warmly – I thereby learned that she was called Irène – and glanced at me triumphantly with the look of a man who has really thought of everything. We talked of this and that, in other words nothing, with the tact that characterizes well-bred people once they are at table. It seems that it only takes a knife, a fork, a plate and the appearance of the first course to induce a kind of discretion in civilized people. On the other hand, no sooner were we on our feet again, or rather seated once more in the drawing room with our coffee, than my future became the subject of renewed discussion. It seemed that I was to live for the time being in the rue Spontini, in Irène's step-daughter's flat; Julius's lawyer, Maître Dupont-Cormeil, would get in touch with Alan and, as a bonus, we would all go the following Saturday to a splendid gala to be given at the Opéra for the Association of Abandoned and Delinquent Pensioners, or something of the kind. I listened to them talking about me as though I were a small child with a sort of incredulity and amused bewilderment that eventually began to worry me. Perhaps I really was this fragile, defenceless, charming, not to say irresponsible young woman it behoved them to take under their wing. There is a certain type of person, to which I belong, who brings out the protector, the parent, in everyone. The fact that you quickly become bored or irritated with these parents, and show it, in no way alters their determination: they simply become the parents of an ungrateful child.

Early in the afternoon we set off for Paris, abandoning the fortified manor to the lugubrious manservant, and by five o'clock I was sitting in the little drawing room in Mme Debout's step-daughter's flat, waiting patiently for Julius's chauffeur to bring me some clothes from home (home being henceforth that grim place, that cage, that snake pit where my weird husband Alan lurked, and which I must avoid for ever more). At eight o'clock, thwarting the plans made by Julius and Mme Debout – plans involving a quiet little dinner for ten in a new restaurant on the Left Bank – I went for a long walk in the rain and ended up by taking refuge with some friends, the Maligrasses, a charming elderly couple long accustomed to my dropping in unannounced. I spent a peaceful night in their house and returned to the rue Spontini the following morning to change my clothes. It was my first escapade and it was ill received.

During the course of the stormy luncheon that followed my return to the fold, I gradually succeeded in putting across my own point of view concerning my future. I wanted to find a bedsitter and a job in order to pay for my food and rent. Mme Debout, no doubt intrigued by my show of resistance, had insisted on joining us for lunch. She tapped her rings on the table and sighed deeply from time to time while Julius looked at me aghast, as though my modest ambitions were a string of absurdities. My old friend Alain Maligrasse had offered to recommend me to the editor of a magazine specializing in music, painting and antiques. It was a small, sedate publication where I should probably be rather badly paid but where my slight knowledge of painting might prove useful. He had also undertaken to get me a job as a reader in the publishing house he worked for, which would supplement my income a little. Mme Debout's sighs grew deeper and deeper, but eventually, seeing that I was adamant and about to give them, or at least Julius, the slip, she tried diplomacy.

'I'm afraid, my dear child,' she said in a pitying voice, 'that all this fascinating work won't get you very far. Financially speaking, I mean. On the other hand,' she went on, turning to Julius, 'if she is absolutely determined to be independent' – she pronounced the adjective in a way that beggars description – 'you must let her. All young women these days have this craze for getting jobs.'

'In my case it's more a matter of necessity,' I said.

She opened her mouth and then closed it again. I knew perfectly well what she was thinking: 'You little fool, you little hypocrite, don't you realize you've got Julius A. Cram behind you . . .' She was actually on the point of saying it aloud but the look on my face, or possibly Julius's slightly alarmed expression, warned her that things were not so simple. An angel, or rather a troupe of demons, passed overhead. Then Julius said:

'I quite understand your attitude. If you'll allow me, I'll get one of my secretaries to find you a suitable flat. That will enable you to go and see these magazine people or anyone else with your mind at rest. In the meantime, it seems to me that you might as well accept Irène's hospitality, since she has offered it.'

I still said nothing and he gave a forced little laugh.

'It won't be for long, I assure you. My secretary is extremely efficient.'

More or less cornered, I gave in.

Julius had not exaggerated when he told me his secretary was efficient. The very next day she arranged for me to look at a two-roomed flat overlooking a courtyard in the rue de Bourgogne that was available at an absurdly low rent. She was a tall young blonde who wore spectacles and an air of resignation. When I congratulated her on what was truly a find, she replied that it was part of her job. And that very same afternoon I was interviewed by Ducreux, the editor of my famous magazine. I had no idea that Alain Maligrasse pulled so much weight in Paris, and I was as surprised as I was delighted when, having asked me a few questions and described what my duties would be, Ducreux engaged me forthwith at a reasonable salary. I rushed round to thank Alain Maligrasse who was just as surprised but no less pleased than I was. No doubt about it, luck was on my side. I left the rue Spontini that same night and moved in. Leaning out of my window, looking down at the flower bed in the courtyard three floors below and listening to a Mahler symphony on the radio which had been kindly lent me by my landlady, I suddenly felt resourceful, independent and absolutely free. It must be said in my defence that I was born naïve and had remained so.

On an impulse, I telephoned Alan. His voice sounded so calm and gentle that I was amazed. I suggested that we should meet at eleven o'clock next morning and he replied 'Yes, fine, I'll expect you here', but I objected strenuously. I saw myself henceforth as one of those super-women one reads about in women's magazines who are miraculously free from nerves and ensure the well-being of husbands, children, bosses and concierges with masterly ease. And this intoxicating image must have given my voice an added firmness, for Alan capitulated and agreed to meet me in an old café in the avenue de Tourville.

I awoke with the same feeling of efficiency and deter-mination, the same impression that I was beginning a new life, and went to keep our appointment. Alan was already there, a cup of coffee in front of him, and he rose to greet me, pushing the table aside and helping me off with my coat in the most natural way possible. Perhaps everything would turn out all right. Perhaps those three weeks of madness and even those three years of paranoia had been merely a bad dream. Perhaps, after all, this young man opposite me, well-shaven, dark-suited, with his courteous manners, would listen to me at last.

'Alan,' I said, 'I've thought it over carefully, and I'm going to live on my own for a while. I've found a job and a flat, and I think it'll be much better this way, for you as well as for me.'

He nodded politely. He appeared to be half-asleep.

'What sort of job?' he asked.

'On a magazine, an arts magazine edited by a friend of Alain Maligrasse. Alain has been terribly kind, you know.'

Luckily I could talk to him about Alain. He was a bit on the old side for there to be any question of jealousy.

'That's pretty good,' he said. 'It didn't take long for you to get fixed up ... or had you been thinking about it for some time?'

'It was a stroke of luck,' I said carelessly, 'or rather a double stroke of luck. The flat and the job.'

He appeared sleepier and more benign than ever.

'Is it a large flat?'

'No,' I said, 'a bedroom, and a sort of sitting room, but it's quiet.'

'And what am I supposed to do about our flat?'

'That's for you to decide. It depends whether you stay in Paris or go back to America.'

'Which would you prefer me to do?'

I squirmed in my chair. I had been expecting Othello and instead I had found Tom Thumb.

'It's up to you,' I said weakly. 'Your mother must miss you, for one thing.'

He began to laugh, with that carefree, youthful laugh of his that up till then I had always thought so spontaneous.

'My mother amuses herself playing bridge or the stock market,' he said. 'And what am I to say to her when I return alone?'

I leant towards him and cautiously placed a hand on his sleeve.

'You can tell her that things haven't worked out too well between us. You don't have to mention divorce straightaway.'

'Am I also to tell her,' said Alan, and his voice was no longer sleepy but had become sibilant and shrill, 'am I also to tell her that I've had my wife taken away from me by a lousy rich old man? God knows you've had enough lovers, Josée, but they used to be a bit better looking, as far as I know. I've never seen anything so sickening as you running away with that grotesque old man on one side and his gorilla of a chauffeur on the other. Since when has he been your lover?'

It was beginning all over again. I should have known. It would always begin again.

'That's completely untrue,' I said. 'You know quite well it isn't true.'

'In that case, by what miracle have you found a job, when you've no qualifications whatsoever? And a flat, when you've never been able to cope with a thing on your own? You disappear without a sou, and two days later you come back triumphantly with a roof over your head and a salaried job. And you expect me to believe you? Do you think I'm a fool?'

A man who had been standing at the bar quite close to us quietly drinking his beer had gradually edged his way further and further from our table. He was now at the other end of the bar watching us, and the waiter was looking at us too, and I realized that Alan was talking too loud. I was so used to his outbursts as well as his whispers that I no longer noticed when he overstepped the mark. He was looking at me with a fury that bordered on hatred. That's what we had come to. And suddenly my modest plans, my praiseworthy ambitions, my new life, all appeared ridiculous, pointless and totally unreal. What was real was this wounded, humiliated, enraged face, the face that for me had long been the face of love itself.

'I'll find you again,' said Alan. 'I'll never leave you alone, you'll never be rid of me. You won't know where I am or what I'm doing, but I'll always turn up in your life just when you think I've forgotten you. And I'll ruin everything.'

I had the feeling that he was putting a curse on me. I was terrified, and then something awoke inside me. Once more I became aware of the walls of this café, the faces of the customers, the bright, cold blue of the sky outside. I grabbed my coat and fled. For a moment I no longer knew where I lived, who I was or what I was supposed to be doing, only that I must get away as fast and as far as possible from that depressing café. I hailed a taxi and told the driver to go to the Étoile: then, once we had crossed the Seine, I pulled myself together and, turning on our tracks, we drove back to the rue de Bourgogne.

For half an hour or more I lay on my bed simply listening to the beating of my heart and gazing at the flowers on the wallpaper. Then I picked up the telephone and rang Julius. He came to collect me and we went and had lunch in a quiet restaurant where he talked to me about his business. I wasn't interested but it did me good. It was the first time I had telephoned Julius of my own accord, and yet it had been almost automatic.

Two months later I was having supper at the Opéra after a performance by a Russian ballet company, comfortably installed between Julius A. Cram and Didier Dalet and listening to the eager chatter of a bunch of Parisian balletomanes. We had reached the dessert stage, and already one writer, two painters and four or five private lives had been torn to shreds.

Didier Dalet listened in silence. He detested these character assassinations and I liked him for it. He was a tall, serious-looking young man and very attractive, but had always fallen for other men who were too handsome, too heartless and too young. He never introduced them to his friends, not because he wished to hide them, but because his tastes inclined him towards roughnecks – real thugs who would have been bored stiff by the dinner parties that his profession and background involved him in. His tormented, unhappy love life apart, his real family was here, among these somewhat cold-hearted people who rather despised him, not for his sexual proclivities but because of the unhappiness they caused him. Nobody in Paris cares what you do provided you're successful, as Balzac was always pointing out, and I thought of Balzac as I looked at my friend Didier's resigned profile. We had become friends by chance, perhaps because my adoption by Julius and Mme Debout had at first been sufficiently dubious in these people's eyes for them to begin by placing me at the bottom of the table, in other words next to him.

We discovered that we both admired certain writers and shared a gift for spontaneity and laughter that made us first of all allies and then, on the strength of further meetings, friends.

My well-regulated existence seemed more agreeable each day. Despite its tiny circulation, the magazine was cheerfully buoyant. Ducreux, the editor, took an interest in my articles, and my time was taken up in flitting from one gallery to another, from one painter to another, alternating between enthusiasm and irritation, but always immersed in the constant stream of paranoid, masochistic and often fascinating gossip that characterized the devotees of the art world. Materially speaking, I managed pretty well for someone unused to having to count the pennies. I must say that my landlady, Mme Dupin, despite her peculiarly avaricious expression, behaved like an angel. Her housekeeper looked after the laundry and the cleaners, and did what little shopping I required, all for a sum as negligible as my rent. The flat was worth three times what I was paying, something that never ceased to astonish me every time I looked at my landlady's predatory mouth and hands. My clothes problems were to all intents and purposes solved by Mme Debout. She knew the owner of a ready-to-wear – I should say ready-to-lend – boutique where I could turn up at any time and choose whatever I liked for that evening, without paying a sou. The proprietor assured me that it was good publicity for him, but in view of my anonymity it was difficult to see how. My being seen in the company of Julius A. Cram couldn't have been the explanation: no newspaper ever mentioned either him or his wealth.

Every other evening, I went out with Julius A. Cram and his merry throng. The rest of the time, I would either visit old friends or else settle down alone and bury myself in some enormous treatise on painting, for I was beginning to take myself seriously in a vague kind of way, and the idea that I might one day help a painter, or, even better, discover a major talent all on my own, didn't seem wholly impossible. In the meantime, I wrote insignificant and rather adulatory articles on equally insignificant and rather likable painters. If, as occasionally happened, someone mentioned one of the pieces I had written, I felt a glow of pride – or rather, perhaps, a kind of vague pleasure – at the idea that I, who had always led a completely useless life could actually, emotional relationships apart, be of help to somebody. And yet it wasn't that I needed to justify myself in my own eyes: all the time I was in love with Alan, during all those years of idleness and lazing about on beaches, I had never had the slightest feeling of guilt. It was only when I ceased to love him, and he knew it, that my life had become this endless misery of which I was so ashamed. In any case, the end of our marriage had been too violent and too painful for me to be able to envisage the possibility of happiness with another man. This job of mine gave a new stability, a new colour to my life. On those evenings when we were alone together, I talked about all this to Julius and he approved. He knew nothing about painting, nor did it interest him, but he admitted as much without pride or shame, which was restful after a day of pretentious chatter. During the past two months, Julius had shown himself in a reassuring light. He was always there when I needed someone to talk to, he took me everywhere without allowing it to appear that there was the slightest intimacy between us, and, notwithstanding my total incomprehension of his true nature, I had come to feel that he was absolutely honourable. From time to time, it is true, I felt his eyes fixed on me in a questioning, insistent manner, and I would simply look away. There was no one else in my life. Alan was still too close, even though he had gone back to America, and if I'd taken home a young critic three evenings in succession, that had been fortuitous. I had probably been scared: you can't share a bedroom with a man for years without from time to time being cruelly surprised at not hearing the echo of another's breathing in the darkness.

On the evening in question, then, cosily ensconced between my rich protector and my unhappy new-found friend, I was placidly watching the party develop when the incident happened. The instigator was a drunken young man, extremely good-looking, a newcomer to our midst whose deliberate insolence gave him a certain cachet. He shouted across to Didier, who, like me a little somnolent, did not at first realize he was being addressed.

'Didier Dalet,' said the young man at the top of his voice, 'someone asked me to give you his love. Your friend Xavier. I met him last night in a place I usually try to avoid. We talked a lot about you.'

Without having met him, I knew who Xavier was and what he meant to Didier. He turned pale and made no reply. A slight silence had fallen at our end of the table, and the young man, emboldened, went on:

'Don't you know who I mean? Xavier!'

Didier still said nothing, as though the 'X' of Xavier was a nail being deliberately driven into his hands or into his memory. At that moment, I'm convinced, he was not in the least concerned about the reaction of the people at our table but was wondering, miserably and angrily, what Xavier had said to this crass young man and how far they had gone in ridiculing him. He shook his head two or three times with a smile of benign bewilderment. But it wasn't enough. All eyes were now turned upon him and the handsome young man pretended to take his headshake for a denial.

'Come now, Monsieur Dalet, doesn't the name Xavier remind you of someone? A dark boy with blue eyes, and not at all bad-looking,' he added, laughing as though he acknowledged that there was some excuse for Didier's tastes.

'I do know someone called Xavier . . .' my friend began in a faint voice, then stopped short.

Mme Debout, who was sitting beside the trouble-maker and, whether deliberately or not, had allowed him to go on uninterrupted, tried to change the subject.

'You're making a great deal of noise,' she said to her neighbour.

The latter was a newcomer, as I have said, and did not realize that a warning from Mme Debout was tantamount to an order: namely to shut up.

'Ah, so you do know a Xavier? We're getting somewhere at last.'

He smiled, delighted with himself, and somebody began to titter inanely, no doubt from embarrassment, and insensibly it rippled round our end of the table. Eight faces, apprehensive but enthralled, confronted the haggard, stricken face of the unfortunate Didier. I saw his hand, exaggeratedly long and white, clutch the tablecloth, but gently, not so much as though to pull it off as to vanish beneath it.

'I know the Xavier you mean very well,' I said in a loud voice. 'He's a great friend of mine.'

Everyone looked at me in amazement. I might be Julius's mistress, I might be Mme Debout's protégée, but I was a young woman who normally kept out of arguments. Momentarily disconcerted, the enemy lost his head and went too far.

'A friend of yours too? Well, well. An intimate friend, no doubt?'

A second later, Julius was standing behind my chair. He didn't say a word. He gave the young man one of those disturbing glances of his that I knew well and we left. I just had time to grab Didier by the arm and drag him from his chair, and the three of us found ourselves in the foyer of the Opéra looking very prim and proper. We collected our coats and were on the way downstairs when one of Mme Debout's bodyguards came running after us.

'You must come back at once. The whole affair is grotesque. Irène is furious.'

'So am I,' said Julius, buttoning his overcoat. 'This lady and gentleman were my guests for the evening.'

Once outside in the fresh air, I burst out laughing, threw my arms around Julius's neck and kissed him. He looked sweet standing there in the cold, with his little navy blue overcoat, his glasses and his few hairs standing on end from anger or the wind. He was irresistible. Didier came close to me and pressed himself gently against me, like an animal that has been whipped without understanding why.

'What bliss to be outside,' I said quickly. 'I couldn't bear that party a moment longer. Julius, your defence of my honour' (I emphasized the 'my') 'has gained us two hours. Let's go and celebrate at Harry's Bar.'

We made our way to the rue Daunou on foot and talked about other things for half an hour, until Didier had regained a bit of colour. There must have been a fine hullaballoo going on at that supper table at the Opéra. It would be a long time before Mme Debout forgave me for creating a scene. It was unheard of for someone to leave her table before she did. Like Dumas's Milady, she was no doubt already plotting her revenge, and if the company of her guests hadn't been a matter of complete indifference to me, I would have slept uneasily that night. Apart from the gratitude I felt towards Julius, there was only one other reason for my presence in their midst: I no longer knew quite what to do with my evenings. The sort of incomunicado existence Alan and I had lived together had made me unaccustomed to physical solitude and had estranged me from my Parisian friends. Moreover, as a couple we were probably attractive enough but exhausting to be with on account of the incessant nervous tension. Then again, my friends had changed during my three-year absence: they now had professional or financial preoccupations that were not as yet mine and that, in my privileged eyes, transformed them from carefree companions into more or less solid citizens. They had rounded the bend into maturity without me, and I had returned among them still an adolescent, accompanied by another adolescent, the idle, well-to-do Alan. We must have irritated them considerably without realizing it. Our characters, pitifully copied from Fitzgerald, had nothing in common with the harsh, punctilious, material world in which they were compelled to struggle by the exigencies of job and family. True, there remained a few carefree and alcoholic failures, a few gentle, resigned souls like the Maligrasses (but they were past the age of competition) and a few nondescript and nostalgic loners whom one almost dreaded meeting. It was doubtless for these reasons that I found Mme Debout's glittering, ferocious and futile little circle almost stimulating. They, at least, had not lost sight of their ambitions: they had never had any other ambition than to belong to that circle and remain in it. They had never had to change costumes.

Next day Didier telephoned me at the magazine, muttered something about the incident of the night before, and asked me to meet him in a bar in the rue de Montalembert of which he was an habitué. He told me he also wanted to introduce me to someone he was very fond of. My immediate thought was that it must be the famous Xavier and I was on the point of refusing, as I disliked getting involved in my friends' private problems, when I told myself that if he wanted us to meet he must after all have some good reason, and I accepted.

I arrived a little early and settled down at a corner table. Then I asked the waiter for an evening paper. A man at the next table leaned over and handed me his with a polite 'Allow me' and I smiled at him as I took it from him. He had a calm face, light brown eyes, a firm mouth and large hands. Something about him suggested a pent-up inner strength as well as a faint disillusionment. He looked at me too, full in the face, and when he assured me that there was absolutely nothing worth reading in the paper, I was immediately convinced of the fact.

'You don't mind waiting?' he asked.

'It depends who for,' I said. 'In this case, it's for a great friend. It doesn't worry me in the least.'

'Shall we talk a bit to pass the time?'

To my great surprise, casual pick-ups not being in my line, five minutes later I found myself talking gaily about politics and films and feeling completely at ease. The quiet way he had of offering me a cigarette, lighting it, smiling, summoning the waiter, made a welcome change from the restless, fidgety gestures of the people I was surrounded with day and night. He made me think of the country. Just at that moment Didier arrived and stopped dead with astonishment at seeing us laughing together.

'I'm so sorry to be late. Do you two know one another?'

Heavens, I thought, can this be Xavier? I could see no connection whatsoever between this man and the young tough Didier had told me about.

'We've just met,' said the stranger.

And Didier introduced us:

'Josée, this is my brother, Louis. Louis, this is my friend Josée Ash whom I've told you about.'

'Oh,' Louis said.

He leant back in his seat and looked at me, I thought, in a less friendly way. This seemed to me absurd, since the brothers were obviously fond of one another. Now I could see a certain resemblance between Didier and the stranger, but the latter's features were more positive and more relaxed; he looked, I thought, like the sort of man Didier would have liked to be.

'You're a friend of Julius A. Cram and Madame Debout,' he said. 'You work on a magazine which I believe is called *Reflections on Art*.'

'You know all about me . . .'

'I've told him a lot about you,' Didier interrupted. 'And I said that we had some good giggles together at some of those parties.'

'Good for you,' said Louis sarcastically. 'Congratulations. Rather Didier than me; he's far better at mixing in that sort of world than I am, and one of us had to. Personally, I've never been able to stand those people. How can you?'

'I hardly know them,' I said, surprised. 'It so happened that Madame Debout and Julius A. Cram did me a good turn a short time ago, and I . . .'

I realized that I was stammering; stammering and apologizing and suddenly furious with myself.

'I know the sort of good turns these people do for you,' he said. 'And I don't like them.'

I flared up.

'That's your privilege.'

'Quite,' he said.

And, to my utter astonishment, I found myself blushing. I felt I really was what people took me for: a woman kept by a rich man, simply because he was rich. This image of myself, which I had detected without flinching in the eyes of several people for the past two months, seemed almost unbearable in the eyes of this particular man. All the same, I wasn't going to say 'Listen, Julius A. Cram is nothing more than a friend. I earn my living and I'm a respectable woman.' I didn't like having to justify myself any more than I liked attacking others.

'You must realize,' I said, 'that it's difficult for a young woman to live on air these days. When my husband left me without a sou, I was only too glad of someone as dependable as Julius A. Cram to lean on.'

And I gave them both a repulsively knowing smile.

'I congratulate you,' said Louis. 'Let's drink to your success.'

'What on earth are you talking about?' Didier exclaimed.

He was utterly at a loss. No doubt he had looked forward to this meeting between his beloved big brother and his best friend of the night before, and now it was a complete and unmitigated flop. I would a thousand times have preferred to meet his Xavier than this malevolent stranger.

'I must be off,' I said. 'I'm going to the theatre tonight, and Julius hates to be late.'

I stood up, shook hands with the elder brother, kissed the younger on the cheek, and made a dignified exit. I walked home, consumed with an irrational fury that nearly caused me to be run over three times by frenzied rush-hour drivers. Suddenly I began to loathe this city of overcast skies, blind motorists, hurrying pedestrians. I began to loathe all the people I had been seeing during the past two months and who until now had seemed merely boring. I began to dread them. Had Alan been around that night, I would certainly have gone back to him, regardless of his jealousy, if only to see the proof of my integrity in someone's eyes.

There was only one person who could come to my rescue, as he had shown the night before, but alas he was the cause of the scandal: Julius. Perhaps he, too, suffered from the fact that people regarded us as lovers when he knew it wasn't true and never would be. But did he really believe it never would be? Or was he taking a calculated risk by placing me and keeping me in a false situation which might one day cease to be false because by then I would have given myself to him out of force of habit and sheer fatigue? Was it conceivable that from his point of view, it was all part of a tacit contract between us? After all, even if to me the idea of any physical relationship between us seemed out of the question, perhaps it didn't to him, and in that case I was behaving unfairly. I began to feel apprehensive. At the same time, a reassuring voice, a voice averse to complications murmured in my ear: 'That's a lot of nonsense. Julius knows quite well that there's no misunderstanding between us. I've never misled him either by word or deed, and just because some puritan scowls at me in a bar, it doesn't mean I have to start questioning a perfectly straightforward friendship.' The trouble was that I recog-

55

nized this voice; it was the voice that had said to me a hundred times: 'Don't let's go into it too deeply; let's just wait and see.' And every night I had seen only too well what chaos and confusion that calm little voice could lead me into. Waiting and seeing, for me, had never produced very brilliant results. No, it was essential that I should talk to Julius, that I should try to clarify matters, and even if it meant making a fool of myself in front of him, at least in future I should feel better in front of the others.

As I arrived home, literally exhausted by my scruples, the telephone rang. It was Didier, of course, a woebegone Didier. 'Josée,' he said, 'what happened? You were so unlike yourself. I thought you'd like Louis and he behaved like a clod.'

'It doesn't matter,' I said.

'Listen, Josée,' Didier went on, 'I know you're not going to the theatre this evening. You told me you were free. Won't you have dinner with me? My brother's left,' he added hastily.

He seemed genuinely distressed. After all, I thought, it would be better to dine with him than to play the tragedy queen all alone. And I could always ask his advice. Confiding in people wasn't my favourite occupation, but it was a long time since I had talked to anyone about myself. I asked him to come round in an hour's time. He came, admired my hidey-hole, and we talked casually about this and that for about twenty minutes until, unable to restrain myself any longer, I poured us two large whiskies and said bluntly, 'Now, let's get down to brass tacks.'

He burst out laughing. He had a delightful, childish laugh and soft eyes. Not for the first time I deplored the fact that fate had not inclined him towards women. He was so full of tact, tenderness and sensitivity. He was my friend. Of the two occasions uppermost in our minds, he began with the one that was, no doubt, the less painful for him. I learnt that his brother was not at all the puritan he seemed but that he had always had a horror of the world he grew up in, that he lived in a remote house in the Sologne and earned his living as a vet. I remembered the countrified impression he had given me. Imagining his large hands on the flanks of a horse, I fell momentarily into a romantic daydream until I remembered that he had taken me for a kept woman. I asked Didier if that was what he thought, in so many words, which startled him.

'A kept woman!' he repeated, 'a kept woman, but of course not!'

'What *do* you think of my relations with Julius? What do other people think?'

'I thought you didn't care what other people thought,' he said weakly.

'Your brother got me on the raw.'

He clasped and unclasped his hands, embarrassed.

'Look,' he said, '*I* know you're not Julius's mistress and that you've no desire to be. But other people think differently. They can't see how you can keep up with their style of life when you work on a little art magazine.'

'All the same, that's how it is,' I said. 'One can manage pretty well in Paris.'

'I suppose so,' he said, as though reluctant to admit it, 'but they think you manage otherwise.'

'And what about Julius?' I said. 'Does he expect something more from me?'

'Of course he does!' he said. 'Julius has made up his mind to get you one way or another, and Julius is a man who never gives up.'

'You don't suppose he's in love with me, do you?'

I must have sounded so incredulous that he laughed.

'I don't know whether he's in love with you, but he wants to keep a hold on you whatever happens,' he said. 'Julius is the most possessive man in the world.'

I gave an agonized sigh and gulped down the rest of my whisky. It certainly seemed my fate in life to be somebody's prey. I'd had enough. Tomorrow, I would have things out with Julius.

Told of my decision, Didier raised his eyes to heaven, and assured me that I wouldn't get a word out of Julius and that it would be a waste of time. 'Having things out,' he added, 'is always a waste of time.' He knew from experience. This led us to talk of Xavier. I learnt a great deal about the refinements of cruelty one man can inflict upon another, far worse than those most women are guilty of. I listened, horrified, as he gave me an account of sleazy bars, jealousies and stabs in the back, a homosexual jungle in which every Christian name resounded like a threat, every vigil like a torture and every act of collusion like a humiliation. What was more, he used terms that were so discreet and euphemistic that they only made his description the more vivid instead of toning it down, and curiously, I recognized in him the same thirst for disaster, the same self-destructive urge that I had found in Alan. It was in himself, and not in the object of his love, that he found his suffering, and perhaps his gratification. It hardly mattered, I now realized, that he loved a man rather than a woman: he would always be unhappy. It was very late when he left, seemingly in better spirits and somewhat assuaged, and I went to bed with a shameful feeling of relief. Whatever became of me, I thought, I would never have that longing for the abyss; whatever happened, I would always wake up some morning or other whistling a jaunty little tune.

The events of the following day, alas, unfolded less to the rhythm of a jaunty little tune than to that of a hesitation waltz. Being in the habit, as I have said, of letting time take its course, I not only distrusted resolutions in general but, in my particular case, was even more mistrustful of the resolutions I took at night than of those I took in the light of day. From prejudice, no doubt, for experience had shown my nocturnal resolutions to be no more catastrophic than those made during the day. In a word, the night, as was its wont, had brought me no relief and I prowled round the telephone trying to persuade myself that I really must have things out with Julius. It wasn't until five o'clock that, in an idle moment, I took the plunge. Without much conviction I told Julius that I needed to see him urgently and alone. He replied that he would send the car for me at six, and sure enough, at six o'clock precisely I set off in the big Daimler which, to make matters worse, took me straight to the Salina. It seemed to be a place that held a strategic importance in Julius's life. He was waiting for me, seated at the same table as three months earlier, and he had already ordered me a rum baba – just as, if I had let him, he would have ordered in every restaurant the grapefruit and entrecote steak I had asked for the first time. I sat down opposite him and momentarily contemplated chatting to him idly about the weather until I remembered that his time was precious, that I had probably thrown out his schedule, and that I must justify my telephone call.

'I'm so sorry to have bothered you, Julius, but I'm rather worried.'

'Whatever it is, I can fix it,' Julius replied confidently.

'I'm not so sure. The thing is, Julius, do you know what people think about us?'

'I don't care what they think,' he said. 'Why?'

I felt somewhat idiotic.

'Well, you must be aware that people are saying that you and I . . .'

'Well . . . what?'

He was beginning to irritate me again. That he was innocent was conceivable, that he was unaware was not.

'They think I'm your mistress,' I said. 'They think you're keeping me and that I'm only interested in your money.'

'Money isn't my only asset,' he retorted with an air of vexation.

Oh God, I thought, I'm going to have to talk to him about his physical charm.

'That's not the point,' I said. 'People really believe it.'

'What do you care what the others think?'

It was an idiosyncrasy common to each individual member of that little set to refer to all the rest as 'the others', as though he or she were a paragon of virtue and a superior intelligence who had strayed into a bunch of contemptible socialites.

'It doesn't bother me,' I said weakly, 'but the last thing I want to do is to upset your private life.'

Julius gave a rather haughty little chuckle that implied that his private life was fine, thank you very much, or else that it was nobody's business but his own. I plunged in deeper.

'Because after all, Julius, you've always been a wonderful friend to me, but I don't suppose you lived alone before you met me. I wouldn't like another woman to think that . . . or be upset because . . .'

This provoked another little chuckle, just as conceited and just as equivocal as the first, from this infuriating tycoon.

'Julius,' I said firmly, 'are you going to answer me?'

He raised his blue eyes to mine and patted my hand patronizingly.

'Don't worry, my dear Josée, when I met you I was a free man.'

Bravo! Any minute now he would turn out to be a world-weary Don Juan whom I'd had the luck to run into in a slack period. This wasn't at all the direction I wanted our conversation to take. Whether it was the décor or the hornets' nest into which I had blundered, I felt as furiously exasperated in this wretched place as on the first occasion.

'Julius,' I said querulously, and I could hear my voice rising to a squeak, 'Julius, people say you never do anything for nothing. As you probably know.'

'They also say that *you* do certain things for money. So?'

Now he was logic-chopping. I could hardly ask him, looking him straight in the eyes, if he had ultimate designs on my person. I sighed, took a mouthful of rum baba, and got out my cigarettes.

'Well now,' said Julius, 'what's all this about, Josée? You know perfectly well that we're friends, and that I have a great affection for you. More than affection, in fact,' he added pensively.

I pricked up my ears.

'I have a great respect for you,' he continued, 'and believe me, it isn't a sentiment that I'm prodigal with. I'm sorry if people are gossiping, but this is Paris. I'm a man, you're a woman – it's only to be expected.'

I was beginning to despair. A few more platitudes and Julius would have me out of sheer exhaustion.

'I'm glad you feel affection and respect for me,' I said. 'And indeed I return those feelings. But Julius, are you sure you haven't contemplated something else?'

'Something else?'

He looked at me, wide-eyed. I felt myself blushing, which was the last straw.

'Yes,' I said, 'something else.'

'Ah, ha!' He laughed gaily. 'My dearest Josée, I never contemplate things, ever. I'm not the contemplative type. I let time sort things out.'

'And where do you think time will lead us?'

'But my dear girl,' he said, smiling – idiotically, I thought – 'the charm of time is that you never know where it will lead you. Never, ever.'

This last bit of wisdom finished me; I gave up the struggle. As Didier had rightly said, I would get nothing out of Julius. In my irritation, I put a cigarette in my mouth the wrong way round and Julius obligingly lit the filter tip. This prompted one of those barking laughs that were his speciality, and he hastened to offer me one the right way up.

'There, you see,' he said, 'you're not making sense. And to think that I was worried just now after your telephone call. No, Josée, trust your friend Julius. Enjoy yourself. Stop thinking so much.'

Now he was talking like the Big Bad Wolf and I felt less and less cut out to be Red Riding Hood. On the other hand, I had to admit that if my fears were unfounded, I had placed Julius in an extremely delicate position. He could hardly say, any more than I could, that the last thing he wished was to share my bed, and perhaps the ambiguity that he allowed to persist was no more than a polite refuge. This thought had no sooner crossed my mind than I adopted it feverishly. It suited me perfectly. After all, it was clear and simple. Thinking back over our conversation, it seemed to me obvious that Julius's attitude was basically that of a man weary of women or disappointed in them. Nowadays, Julius was primarily interested in power and his business affairs and only secondarily in a likable young woman whom he was trying to help. All the rest was a figment of my imagination and of Didier's, whose exacerbated sensibility saw violent emotions everywhere. I breathed again, though not without a slight constriction. But after all, I had done what I could within the bounds of ridicule and honesty. And if Julius had any sinister intentions, my uneasiness and rebellion must have given him fair warning. I brightened up. We reminisced about the evening at the Opéra; I congratulated Julius on his prompt reaction, he congratulated me on my presence of mind, we spoke affectionately of Didier and irreverently of Mme Debout, and he dropped me back home. In the car, he tucked my arm beneath his and patted my hand, chatting away as gaily as a schoolboy. Upon reflection, I felt a little ashamed at having attributed such machiavellian designs to this awkward but honourable man. Disinterestedness was not an empty word. It was too bad if Didier's big brother, for all his good looks and large hands, hadn't the wit to understand that much. It was easy to sneer and condemn, a little too easy. Tomorrow, I would talk it over with Didier and try to make him revise his judgement. No question, I had been absolutely right to have qualms about launching into that absurd confrontation. One should always follow one's instinct. The only trouble was that in my case my instincts were so contradictory. The next time I found myself at the Salina, I would taste that rum baba properly. I still couldn't decide whether it was delicious or uneatable.

The concierge stopped me on my way upstairs and handed me a telegram. It said that Alan was very ill and I was to come to New York at once; a ticket in my name was awaiting me at Orly. It was from Alan's mother. I telephoned New York right away and got her butler. Yes, Mr Ash was in hospital; no, he didn't know the reason;

and Mrs Ash did indeed expect me as soon as possible. So it wasn't a trick: his mother hated me too much, as she hated anyone who might have loved her son, to associate herself with a lover's lie. I stood there panic-stricken, my heart thumping, in the middle of my room surrounded by my art magazines, in a setting that suddenly seemed unreal. Alan was ill, Alan might die. The thought was unbearable. Whether or not New York was a trap, I must go there at once. I telephoned Julius, who was magnificent. He found me a flight leaving in four hours' time, booked me a seat, came to collect me, and drove me to the airport, all with the utmost equanimity. When I said good-bye to him, at the passport control, he told me not to worry. He himself had to be in New York the following week and he would arrange to put forward his journey. In any case he would telephone me the next morning at the Pierre Hotel where he kept a permanent suite and where he suggested I should stay. It would reassure him to know where he could find me. I agreed to everything, comforted by his kindness, his calm and his efficiency. Seeing him from the distance, a tiny figure waving to me from the other side of the barrier, I felt I was leaving behind a very dear friend. In three months he had really become, in the truest sense of the word, a protector.

In the huge aircraft speeding imperturbably across the night and the ocean, all the passengers were asleep and I sat alone in the bar on the upper deck, the little bar so like an independent rocket that one almost expected it to detach itself from the plane and take off on its own into the galaxy. The last time I had made this journey, two years before, it had been daylight and in the opposite direction, and the plane had flown through pink and blue clouds in pursuit of the sun. Then, I was running away from Alan, and all the brutal, monstrous power of the machine was taking me further and further from him, whom in spite of everything I still loved. Now that same power was bringing me as obediently back to the same Alan – whom I no longer loved. I was at ease in this empty bar, where a sleepy barman, cursing me no doubt, would appear from time to time to offer me a whisky which I refused. It had certainly been an excellent idea on the part of my mother-in-law to buy me that first-class ticket which alone gave access to the bar – indeed, to buy me a ticket at all. It suggested that she knew I was penniless. What would she make of that? True, as Alan's mother, and a possessive one to boot, she could hardly be expected to wish me comfortably off. But as an American, an American woman, she must be shocked at Alan's having left me unprovided for. Two divorces and a bereavement had made her rich, and for her, women's rights in this field were no laughing matter. I wondered how Alan had managed to explain things.

She was a hard, possessive woman whose handsome profile, twenty years earlier, had been compared by *Harper's Bazaar* to that of a bird of prey. This description had delighted her, no one knew why, and she had even adopted certain neck movements and an occasional unblinking stare that accentuated the resemblance still further. In the early days of our marriage she had attempted to fascinate me, but I was in love with Alan and knew him to be unhappy, and instead of an eagle I saw only a bad-tempered old hen. Her various manoeuvres to separate us had only helped to bring us closer together and to make us avoid her. We alone were responsible for the demolition of our marriage. Nevertheless it was thanks to her that I was on this plane, and I realized that from now on all the sunlight, all the clouds, all the beautiful landscapes which the earth, spread out, below me had proffered for my delectation, all the glamorous daydreams engendered by all those frequent flights would now be subordinated to my new standard of living, in other words, severely restricted. My freedom, my precious freedom, would gradually prove to be limited on all sides. I did not dwell for long on these melancholy thoughts; drowning the roar of the engines and the clink of ice cubes in my glass, an incessant drumming inside my skull reminded me that Alan was ill, perhaps dying, and that somehow or other it was my fault. I didn't sleep a wink and arrived at the PanAm terminal exhausted. The airport too had changed. It was bigger, more glittering, more frightening than I remembered it, and I was suddenly as afraid of this overpowering country as if I were a complete stranger to it. The cab driver and I were now separated by a pane of opaque glass, bullet proof and thus also proof against the cheerful and relaxed conversations I remembered. And the further we drove into that city of stone and concrete, the more it seemed that all the cab windows were equally opaque and unbreakable, cutting me off for ever from the New York I loved so much. Needless to say, my mother-in-law lived on Central Park and the hall porter telephoned her apartment before allowing me up. New York, too, had become a barricaded city. I vaguely recognized the icy entrance hall, the walls smothered in abstract paintings, each one an investment, and walked, shivering, into the drawing room. The bird of prey was there and she swooped down upon me. She kissed my cheek with such a sharp peck that for a moment I feared she might have removed a morsel of flesh. Then she held me at arm's length and looked at me.

'You don't look well . . .' she began.

I cut her short:

'How is Alan?'

'Don't worry,' she said. 'He's all right. Or at any rate he's alive.'

I sat down abruptly, my legs trembling. I must have looked very pale, because she rang and asked the butler to bring some cognac. How strange, I thought, as the terrifying contractions of my heart subsided, how strange that one should be offered whisky as a restorative in France and brandy in America. I felt so relieved that I would cheerfully have discussed the point with my mother-in-law, but it wasn't the moment. I swallowed the contents of the glass, and felt myself reviving. I was in New York, I was sleepy, Alan was alive and that eight-hour journey had been no more than a nightmare, one of those ferocious and senseless slaps in the face that life administers quite gratuitously from time to time. I gazed through a sort of fog at this well-groomed woman sitting opposite me and listened to her talking to me about neurosis and depression, about over-indulgence in alcohol, over-indulgence in amphetamines and tranquillizers, what was, in fact, over-indulgence in passion. Then she remembered my fatigue, my journey, and I allowed myself to be led to my room where I collapsed on the bed fully dressed. Briefly I heard the incessant, diffused hum of the city before I fell asleep.

He did indeed look ill, my beach companion, my partner in pleasures and torments. He had two days' growth of beard, his cheeks were sunken and his eyes glassy, none of which surprised me considering the treatment the psychiatrists must have been inflicting upon him. In this glossy, sound-proofed, air-conditioned little room, he looked like a joke in bad taste, or an outlaw. The precise and pedantic doctor who greeted us had talked of a marked improvement but of the need for surveillance, and it seemed to me that after having brought something human, however painful it may have been at times, into the life of this man who was still such a child, I had failed him and sent him back into a sterilized nightmare. He had taken my hand and was gazing at me, neither pleadingly not aggressively but with a quiet relief that was worse than any outburst. He seemed to be saying: 'Look, I've changed, I've realized, I'm livable-with again, so you can take me back.' For a moment I felt so sorry for him what with his too attentive mother and his too remote psychiatrist that I almost believed it might work. Yes, this was worse than anything. He had the look of a whipped but trusting dog, a look that said that his punishment had gone on long enough, had been thorough enough, and that only my cruelty prevented me from getting him out of this hellish place. The room was bleak in the extreme. Where were the fitted carpets on which he was in the habit of stretching out his long limbs? Where were the cashmere scarves with which he used to cover his eyes, on bad days, in order to sleep? Where was the easy-going life, the bed of roses that the narrow streets of Paris, the little deserted cafés and the silence of the night represented for him? As I well knew, the dull throb of New York never ceased, day or night, something he must have found intolerable at first. But now the silence of this room, this artificial deathly silence, must seem even crueller. 'I've been here a week,' he said, meaning 'Do you realize what it's like? Do you?' 'They're very polite,' he added, meaning 'Can you imagine me, *me*, at the mercy of these strangers?' 'That doctor's not too bad,' he admitted, meaning, 'Why have you abandoned me to this soulless stranger?' And when he finally murmured 'I'll be out in a week, I should think,' I could hear him silently screaming, 'A week, only a week, wait just one week for me!' I was being literally torn apart and, of course, it was the happy memories of our life together that tormented me: our laughter, our arguments, our siestas on the beach, our mutual abandon and, above all, those unforgettable moments of certainty – the certainty that we loved one another and that we should grow old together. I forgot the nightmare of the past two years, I forgot that other certainty, which had been mine alone, that to go on as we were was to head for disaster. I promised him I would come back the next day at the same time. Outside, on Park Avenue, the din and bustle appalled me, and instead of setting off on foot and trying to renew my acquaintance with New York, I made a dive for the interior of my mother-in-law's car. She suggested that we go and have tea at the San Regis, where it would be quiet, and I agreed. I seemed destined to spend the rest of my life in chauffeur-driven limousines and tea rooms in the company of people twice as old as I and ten times more self-assured. This time, however, I ordered a whisky and to my great surprise my mother-in-law did likewise. That hospital must have been exceptionally depressing. I felt a fleeting sympathy for her. Alan was her only son and, despite that bird of prey profile, it was possible that a mother's heart beat beneath her Saint Laurent plumage.

'How do you think he looks?'

'As you said: perfectly well and perfectly awful.'

There was a silence and I could tell that, after her momentary weakness, she was sharpening her weapons.

'My dear Josée,' she said, 'I've always tried not to interfere in your lives.'

That was a lie to begin with, but clearly there were more to come so I let it pass.

'So I have no idea,' she went on, 'why you've separated. Anyway I wanted you to know that I was quite unaware that Alan had gone off leaving you without a cent. By the time I found out, he was really ill and it was too late to take him to task about it.'

I made a gesture with my hand to signify that it was of no importance, but since she didn't share this opinion, she made a sharp counter gesture to signify that on the contrary it was. We looked like a couple of maritime signallers using different codes.

'How have you been managing?' she asked.

'I've found a job, not terribly well paid, I'm afraid, but quite interesting.'

'And who is this Mr Cram? You know, I had an awful job the other day getting your address out of his secretary.'

'This Mr Cram, as you call him, is a friend of mine,' I said. 'That's all.'

'Is that all?'

I looked up. I must have shown my annoyance because she seemed to accept, temporarily at least, that that was all. I suddenly remembered that I had promised Julius to be at the Pierre and to telephone him, and I felt rather guilty. France, Julius, the magazine, Didier, all seemed so far away and the petty complications of my Parisian life so unimportant that I felt doubly lost. Lost in this terrifying city, face to face with this hostile woman, after that sinister clinic, lost, rootless, loveless and friendless, lost even in my own eyes. And the customary tumbler of iced water placed on the table in front of me, the indifferent waiter, the noise from the street, all these left me shivering in my chair, my hands on the table, gripped by an unbearable misery and despair.

'What do you intend to do?' my implacable companion asked severely, and with the utmost sincerity I answered 'I don't know.'

'You must make a decision about Alan,' she said.

'I've made it. Alan and I must get a divorce. I told him so.'

'That's not what he told me. According to him, you decided to try to live apart for a time, but there was nothing final about it.'

'It was final, nevertheless.'

She looked at me intently. One of her more maddening habits was to stare at you for a long while, like a hypnotist, on occasions which she imagined to be moments of truth. I shrugged my shoulders and looked away, which annoyed her and brought out all her spleen.

'Listen to me, Josée. I've always been against this marriage. Alan was so sensitive and you so independent that he was bound to suffer. If I sent for you, it was solely because he had asked for you, and because I found about twenty letters in his bedroom that he had written to you and stamped but not posted.'

'What did they say?'

She fell into the trap.

'He wrote that it was impossible for him to . . .'

She stopped dead, realizing that she had stupidly given herself away, and if she hadn't been so heavily made-up, I'm sure I would have seen her blush.

'All right,' she muttered, 'so I read his letters. I was desperately worried and I felt it my duty to open them. As a matter of fact, that was how I learned of Mr Cram's existence.'

She was recovering her arrogance. God knows what

Alan might have written on the subject of Julius. I felt an upsurge of invigorating anger that jerked me out of my misery. The image of Alan lying in bed, helpless, his eyes blurred, slowly faded. There was no question of my spending another day with this woman who hated me. I refused to put up with it. On the other hand, I had promised Alan to go back the following day, and that was a promise I intended to keep.

'Apropos of Julius A. Cram,' I said, 'he very kindly offered to lend me his suite at the Pierre. So there's no need for me to trouble you any longer.'

She gave me a little smile at this news and made a little bow as if to say 'Bravo, my girl, we don't seem to be managing too badly.'

'You're no trouble at all,' she said. 'All the same, I guess a suite at the Pierre is more fun for you than your mother-in-law's apartment. You see what I meant by your independence.'

She was wearing a blue and black hat, a sort of beret covered with birds of paradise, and I suddenly longed to pull it down over her face, as in one of those film comedies, and leave her sitting there, blindly expostulating, in the middle of the tea lounge. Whenever I lose my temper, there always comes a moment when I'm overcome by an absurd, frantic desire to laugh and might do anything. It's my alarm signal. I rose hurriedly and went to collect my coat.

'I'll go and see Alan tomorrow as arranged,' I said. 'I'll get the Pierre to send someone for my suitcase. About the divorce, a Paris solicitor will be getting in touch with yours. I'm sorry to have to leave you so suddenly,' I added – prompted by a reflex of good manners dating from childhood – 'but I must telephone my friends and my office in Paris before it's too late.'

I held out my hand and she took it, looking for once a little haggard, asking herself perhaps whether she hadn't gone too far, whether I might complain to Alan about her and whether Alan would be furious with her for it.

'All this is between ourselves,' I said, cursing myself for my compassion, and I turned on my heel.

She called my name very loudly and I stopped. Perhaps, by some miracle, she was about to talk to me like a human being.

'About your suitcase,' she said, 'don't trouble yourself. My chauffeur will bring it round to the Pierre in an hour or so.'

The receptionist at the Pierre seemed very relieved to see me. He had been expecting me all day and was afraid that the flowers in my room might have wilted a bit. Mr Julius A. Cram had telephoned twice from Paris and left a message to say that he would ring again at eight o'clock New York time, meaning two in the morning in Paris. Julius's suite was on the thirteenth floor and consisted of two bedrooms separated by a vast sitting room, all furnished in Chippendale. It was seven o'clock in the evening, and going across to the window I suddenly recovered that sense of enchantment I thought I had lost. New York was a blaze of lights. By night, the city became glittering and phantasmal once more, and having miraculously succeeded in opening the fanlight, I lingered by the window to enjoy the evening breeze; it smelt of sea, dust, petrol, and was as much a part of New York as the continual background noise. It was a smell I never grew tired of. Then I sat down on a sofa, switched on the television set and was immediately plunged into a western and deafened by gunfire and righteous sentiments. If there was one thing I needed just then, after that depressing afternoon, it was to be taken out of myself. But the strange thing was that whenever a horse crashed to the ground, I crashed with it, when a villain received a bullet in the heart, I received it too, and the love scenes between the pure young girl and the re-formed tough guy seemed to me like personal affronts. I switched on another channel and got a thoroughly sadistic thriller which bored me. I turned off the set and waited for eight o'clock. I must have been a comic sight, sitting there alone on that sofa with nothing to do, dwarfed by all that space: I must have looked like a well-heeled immigrant. My suitcase had arrived but I had neither the energy nor the desire to unpack. I could feel the blood beating idiotically at my wrists, at my temples, with a regular pulsation that was as remorseless as it was pointless. At five past eight the telephone rang and I rushed to answer it. Julius's voice sounded very clear and very close and it seemed to me that my last remaining link with the living world was that telephone cable snaking beneath the ocean in defiance of storm and tempest.

'I've been worried,' Julius said. 'Where have you been?'

'I arrived very early at my mother-in-law's, or rather very late, and I slept all morning at her apartment. Then I went to see Alan.'

'How is he?'

'Not very well,' I said.

'Are you thinking of coming back soon?'

I hesitated; my mind was a blank.

'Because I could be in New York tomorrow,' he said. 'I have a few things to sort out and then I'm going to Nassau, also on business. If you like, you could come with me and my secretary. A week in the sun wouldn't do you any harm.'

A week in the sun. I imagined a white beach, an indigo sea and a blazing sun to warm my weary bones. I'd had enough of cities.

'What about Ducreux?' I said. 'My boss?'

'I telephoned him as we arranged. He thinks you should take advantage of your stay in New York to see one or two exhibitions – he's given me the names. I'm sure he'll agree to your being away if you bring him back a few articles. He even seemed to think that your trip was a stroke of luck.'

I felt restored to life. This utterly futile and gloomy trip was turning out to be useful, perhaps even interesting, with the additional and unlooked-for pleasure of finding myself on a beach once more. I didn't know Nassau. Alan and I had always sought out the smaller, remote islands off Florida or in the Caribbean. But I knew that Nassau was a tax haven and it was hardly surprising that Julius should have set up one of his outposts there.

'That would be ideal,' I said.

'It would do us both good,' Julius went on. 'The weather here is abominable, and I'm exhausted.'

I couldn't imagine Julius exhausted or even depressed. I tended to think of him as a bulldozer, but that was no doubt unfair of me, or unimaginative, which is often the same thing.

'I'll be there as soon as I can,' he continued. 'Don't you bother about me. What are you doing this evening?'

I hadn't the least idea and said so. He laughed and advised me to go to bed and watch a film to put me to sleep. He told me to ask for a Mr Martin at the reception desk who would look after me, gave me news of Didier who, it seemed, was missing me already, pointed out that there were some amusing books in his bedroom, wished me good night affectionately – in short, reassured me.

I ordered a light supper from room service, found a book by Malaparte in the other bedroom, and took advantage of my good mood to unpack. A few blocks from my hotel, a broken young man, stretched out in the silence of his hospital room, longed for the night to be over. For a moment I thought of that long wait in the dark, and that agonized profile, or rather that unshaven face buried in the pillow, then I plunged into my book and forgot everything except the baroque and savage world of *Kaput*. It had been a hard day.

The next morning, before going to the clinic, I went to

an exhibition of Edward Hopper, an American painter whom I particularly admired. I spent an hour lost in contemplation of those melancholy canvases, people with solitary figures. I paused longest in front of a picture entitled 'The Sea Watchers', in which a man and a woman, sitting side by side but indubitably strangers to each other, gazed out to sea, a cube-shaped house behind them. It seemed to me that here, in a nutshell, was a cruel illustration of the life Alan and I had led together.

He had shaved, there was a little more colour in his cheeks, and the panic-stricken, imploring gleam in his eyes had disappeared. It had been replaced by a different gleam which I recognized at once: one of anger and distrust. He barely gave me time to sit down.

'So, I gather you've left the apartment and are living in Julius A. Cram's suite. Did he come here with you?'

'No,' I said. 'He lent me the suite, and since your mother and I don't get on, as you know . . .'

He interrupted me. His cheeks glowed and his eyes sparkled. It struck me, sadly, not for the first time, that jealousy did wonders for his looks. There is a strange race of people, more numerous than one might expect, who find strength and self-possession only in battle.

'I was stupid enough to think,' he said, 'that you had come specially to see me, but I might have realized that *he*'s not such a fool as to leave you on your own for more than a couple of days. When's he coming?'

I was infuriated. That damnable intuition of his, half true, half false, made it impossible for me to convince him that I was telling the truth. I was back in the same hopeless situation I had been in all through our marriage, always suspected, never innocent. I tried to laugh it off, chatting about Hopper, about New York, about my flight, but he wouldn't listen. In no time he was back in the groove of his past grievances, and I told myself with a mixture of fury and relief that I had been right all along, that it was inevitable that we must leave one another, and that yesterday's brief interview which had left me so vulnerable, so full of tender feeling, had been fortuitous, an accident inspired by pity. And I knew only too well that pity was no basis for an emotional relationship unless at the risk of gradual asphyxia and degradation.

'Anyway,' I said in a last attempt at conciliation, 'you know perfectly well that there's nothing physical between Julius and me.'

'True,' he said, 'you usually went for the better-looking ones in my day.'

'I didn't go for anyone, as you put it, in your day. There were precisely two lapses, both provoked by you.'

'At any rate, Julius A. Cram has taken you under his wing, his golden wing, and you seem to be enjoying it. And besides,' he added with sudden violence, 'what difference does it make to me whether you sleep with him or not! You see him constantly, you talk to him, you telephone him, you smile at him, yes, you smile and talk to someone else, not me! Even if he's never laid a finger on you, it comes to the same thing.'

'Do you want us to go through those last few weeks together again? Start living like raving lunatics again? Is that your life's dream?'

His eyes never left me.

'Yes,' he said. 'I had you completely to myself for a whole fortnight, just as I had you to myself on those deserted beaches I took you to, where you didn't know a soul. Except that after a fortnight you'd made friends among the fishermen, the tourists, or the waiters, and we had to leave. The Virgin Islands, and Barbados, and the Galapagos are finished for us, but there are still islands left that you don't know, and I'll drag you there by force if I have to!'

He was yelling, sweating, going really berserk. I got up from my chair, appalled. A nurse came in, calmly but swiftly, armed with a syringe. Then, as Alan went on struggling, she rang the bell and a male nurse appeared and motioned me to leave. I stood leaning against a wall in the corridor, like someone in a novel, with a terrible desire to vomit. Alan went on shouting the names of exotic islands, Brazilian beaches, Indian provinces, in a voice that grew ever more piercing, and I blocked my ears. Suddenly there was silence, and the nurse emerged from the room with the same perfectly calm face.

'He's in a fine state,' she said, and it seemed to me that her look was full of reproach.

I had had enough; I couldn't stand any more; I turned on my heel and stumbled back through the now silent hospital. Whatever Alan might say, I would never see him again; it was impossible, impossible, and those four syllables haunted me until I reached the suite in the Pierre. I opened the door. Julius's secretary, who was opening some luggage, looked at me with alarm, then Julius came out of his room and I fell on his shoulder and wept. As he was shorter than me, I had to bend down a little in order to lean against him, and in silhouette, we must have resembled some strange exotic house-plant, drooping but propped up by a sharp and very sturdy little wooden stake.

The beach at Nassau was smooth and white, the sun was hot, the water warm and clear. I recited all this to myself like an incantation, lying in a hammock and trying to believe the evidence of my eyes. I was not succeeding. I felt no pleasure, not even physical, in the sum of all these blessings. Ever since my arrival three days before, a sort of insidious insect had been running around inside my skull repeating 'What are you doing here? What's the use? You're alone.' And yet I had experienced on occasion, precisely when alone, those moments of extraordinary, almost metaphysical happiness, when one suddenly discovers in a single dazzling, concrete flash that life is a wonderful thing, that it is completely, incontrovertibly justified, in that precise instant, by the simple fact of being alive. My other moments of happiness had been shared, and certainly seemed to have been the more numerous; as if the conjunction of two pairs of eyes were needed to detect and focus on that microscopic molecule of happiness. At present, my own eyes hadn't the strength to recreate that dazzling light unaided. Julius, who disliked the heat, talked business in one of the hotel's luxurious air-conditioned reception rooms, and when we met for meals with Mlle Barot, he would compliment me on my tan. He himself was very pale and run down. He took quantities of different pills, white, yellow and red, with which he had stocked up in New York and which from time to time, with an imperious gesture, he would demand from poor Mlle Barot who would give him an anxious glance. Personally, I had a superstitious fear of medicaments, but I refrained from alluding to them out of a prudishness that was thoroughly old-fashioned these days when everyone enthusiastically described their smallest symptoms. Nevertheless, this morbid appetite for pills seemed to me disquieting, and I finally interrogated Mlle Barot who, somewhat stiffly, reeled off a horrifying list of pep pills, sleeping pills and tranquillizers. I was astonished. Did Julius, the powerful and invulnerable tycoon, need tranquillizers? Was my protector himself hungering for protection? The world was upside down. Yet I knew that nine-tenths of the 'well-nourished population' of the globe had recourse to these aids. It was natural that Julius, a lonely man weighed down with business worries, should feel the need for them. Nevertheless, it was the first sign of weakness he had displayed, and it frightened me. All the same, I was old enough to know that there is always sand beneath the concrete, or concrete beneath the sand, and that the difficulty of being is universal, and I began to wonder about Julius's childhood, his inner life and his true nature. It was high time: I ought to have taken an interest in someone who had been so good to me a little sooner.

Apart from this brief moment of remorse, I was bored to death in Nassau, which was a caricature of itself, packed with hysterical American women and worn-out businessmen. Luckily, thanks to the competition of innumerable swimming pools safe from sharks and microbes, the sea was deserted. Being alone on the beach day in, day out, even though it got me down at times, numbed me a little, dulled the echo of Alan's yells in his hospital room, and I waited without too much impatience either for my body to become completely attuned to its surroundings or for our return to Paris. The evenings were particularly beautiful, with tables set overlooking the sea, and an invisible pianist accompanied by a bongo group playing Cole

Porter favourites in the shadows. After dinner, a handful of hotel guests would lie in hammocks and watch the reflections of sea and moon merge in the never-ending murmur of the waves. It was on one such evening, Julius having expressed the incongruous wish for a Strauss waltz, that I sought out the pianist on his wooden platform at the water's edge. I made my request in a rather flustered voice because he was strikingly handsome: very brown, very slim, very nonchalant, very sure of himself, and our eyes met in one of those undisguised looks that I have exchanged with a stranger only a few times in my life, looks that had sometimes led to something and sometimes not, but which were on each occasion a clear recognition signal. He launched into the Viennese waltz and I walked quickly away, smiling at my misconduct, past or future, and thereupon forgot him. But for a moment that look made me feel once again that I was a woman, desirable and alive.

And then, the next day, Julius collapsed on the beach. He had come up to my hammock, had murmured something about the heat, and suddenly fell forward. He lay sprawled at my feet, in his neat blue blazer and tie and his grey flannel trousers – fortunately, he firmly eschewed the bermuda shorts and tee shirts sported by the few, over-weight, hotel guests – and that small, sombre figure, lying on the sparkling sand, seemed to me for a moment like something out of a surrealist painting. I hurried to his aid, someone else came running up, and together we carried Julius up to his room. The doctor spoke of overwork and tension, and with Mlle Barot I waited for an hour until he recovered a little. When he asked for me, I went in and sat on the end of his bed, filled with pity as for a sick child. In his pale grey pyjamas whose open neck revealed a completely hairless chest, his blue eyes blinking tremulously without his glasses, he seemed so defenceless, so much like an elderly little boy, that for a moment I felt guilty for not having brought him a toy or some sweets to comfort him.

'I'm so sorry,' he said. 'I must have given you a fright.'

'You certainly did,' I admitted. 'You must rest, Julius, get out on the beach, go for a swim.'

He blushed.

'I've always been terrified of water,' he said. 'To tell you the truth, I can't swim.'

He looked so chagrined that I began to laugh.

'Tomorrow,' I said, 'I'll give you a lesson in the swimming pool. In any case, no more work for you today; you're going to come and settle down quietly in a hammock next to me and look at the sea. You don't even know what colour it is.'

I felt rather like a social worker, but he nodded feebly, delighted that for once someone else was taking the decisions. Dependence, like its opposite, must be a fundamental human need. With the doctor's permission and Mlle Barot's help, we installed Julius with his rug in a large rope hammock that almost swamped him. I settled down beside him and opened my book, since I imagined that he was tired and would prefer not to talk.

'Are you going to read?' he asked at once in a plaintive voice.

'No, no,' I said, with obvious insincerity, and closed my book.

I was going to have to talk to him. I was about to give him a brief sermon on the abuse of drugs, but I was interrupted by the same plaintive voice. All I could see of him was a tuft of hair, the rug, and his hands gripping the sides of the hammock as though he were in an unstable canoe.

'Are you bored here?'

'Of course not,' I said. 'Why should I be? This place is lovely and I adore doing nothing.'

'I'm always afraid that you may be bored,' Julius said. 'If I believed you were, it would be terrible for me.'

'But why?' I interrupted brightly.

'Because since I've known you, I've never been bored myself.'

I murmured 'That's nice' in a reticent voice. I was beginning to dread what was coming.

'Since I've known you,' Julius's voice continued, his voice muffled either by shyness or by the rug, 'since I've known you. I no longer feel alone. I've always been a very lonely person, through my own fault, I suppose. I don't know how to talk to people: either I frighten them or else I put them off. Women especially. In their opinion, what I want is either too simple or not good enough. Or perhaps I'm not good enough when it comes to women. I don't know.'

I said nothing.

'Or else,' he went on with a deprecating laugh, 'I've only come across women who aren't good enough. And then I've always been so preoccupied with my work. In business you see, you can never relax. Unless you keep an eye on things, they go wrong, you always have to be on the spot and ready to take decisions, even when you've lost interest. I often wonder why one bothers.'

'A lot of people depend on you, so it's natural for you to be concerned.'

'They may depend on me,' he said, 'but I don't depend on anyone. I'm my own boss. As I told you, I was poor at one time, and I don't think I was any lonelier then, or any more unhappy.'

The sad little voice emerging from the oversized hammock filled me with an unexpected tenderness and pity. I tried hard to reassure myself, to recall the formidable business tycoon I had known in Paris, with his piercing eyes and rasping voice, but I could only think of the little man in navy blue whom I had seen collapse in the heat of the sun an hour or two before.

'Why have you never married?' I asked.

'I only ever wanted to once. To that English girl, if you remember. It took me a long time to get over that, and then later, it was too easy. Being so rich, you see . . .'

'There must have been women who loved you for other reasons,' I said.

'I doubt it. Or maybe I did them an injustice.'

There was a silence, and I tried desperately to find something to say to him that wasn't hopelessly banal or stupidly encouraging, but I could think of nothing.

'That's why,' Julius went on, his voice getting lower and lower, 'since I've known you, I've been so much happier. I have the feeling of looking after you, of having someone to care for at last. And it's a hard thing to say, but when you came back to the Pierre the other day, when you burst into tears and allowed me to comfort you, well, I know it's dreadful, but I hadn't been so happy for a long time.'

I said nothing. I sat there quite motionless. I could feel a drop of perspiration running down my back, and I shut my eyes, as though by being unable to see I could avoid hearing. At the same time I realized, with a sort of savage self-contempt, that ever since our first meeting at the Alferns', ever since the moment I had found myself face to face with Julius A. Cram, I had been expecting this. My honesty was really hypocrisy, my nonchalance blindness.

'The fact is,' Julius said, 'I couldn't bear to lose you.'

There could be no question of my retorting that, having nothing, there was nothing he could lose. It was with him that I had come on this holiday, with him that I spent nearly every evening, and when things went wrong, it was to him that I turned, on him that I relied. The absence of physical possession did not prohibit him from feeling a sense of moral possession, perhaps made that feeling even stronger. It was cruel and stupid to deny that it was perfectly possible to share someone's life without sharing their bed – even if it was unfashionable, and God knows it was that. In fact, I felt a greater responsibility towards Julius, in refusing him that false gift, the facile, temporary loan of my body, than towards a lot of men to whom I had given it. I made a final attempt at lightheartedness:

'But there's no question of your losing me, Julius . . .'

He interrupted me.

'I should like you to know that I desperately want to marry you.'

I sat bolt upright in my hammock, horrified at the word, the tone of voice, the idea, horrified by the fact that this utterance demanded a reply on my part, that my reply would be no and that I didn't want to hurt him. And once more I felt terrified and guilty, a hunted creature surrounded by the pitiless weapons of feelings I didn't share.

'Don't answer now,' Julius said hurriedly, and I could tell by his voice that he was as terrified as I was. 'I'm not asking you for anything, especially not for an answer. I simply wanted you to know.'

With a feeling of cowardly relief I lay back in my hammock, got out my cigarettes and suddenly realized that the pianist had been playing for some time. Now I recognized the tune: it was *Mood Indigo* and unconsciously I tried to remember the words.

'I'm going to bed,' Julius said. 'Forgive me, but I'm a little tired. I'll have dinner in my room.'

I murmured 'Good night, Julius' and he walked away with his rug over his arm, leaving the sand, the sea and his love at my feet, and me completely demoralized.

An hour later, I went into the empty bar and swallowed two Planters' Punches. Ten minutes later, the pianist came in and asked if he could offer me another. Half an hour later, we knew one another's Christian names, and an hour later, I was naked beside him in his bungalow. For an hour I forgot everything; then I went back to my room stealthily, like the woman taken in adultery. I wasn't proud of myself, by any means. But nor did I deceive myself: the fulfilment I felt in my body was no less real than the famine I felt in my heart.

Paris was dazzling on this first evening of spring. The golds and blues of its façades were as elusive as the light that bathed them. Its bridges seemed suspended in midair, its monuments floating, its pedestrians winged. In my euphoria, I went into a florist's shop and a basset hound came running up to me, barking. It appeared to be alone in charge of the establishment. After a few minutes, when no one had come, I asked the dog the price of the tulips and the roses. I walked round the shop pointing out pot-plants to him and he followed me, yapping, obviously delighted with this new game. I was discoursing enthusiastically on the merits of the daffodils when someone knocked on the window. I turned and saw a man standing on the pavement, smiling and tapping his forehead ironically with his index finger. My pantomime with the dog for the past five minutes must have looked pretty absurd, and I smiled back at him. We looked at one another through the superfluous plate glass flooded with sunlight and, while the basset hound barked more furiously than ever, Louis Dalet pushed open the door and took my hand in his. He was even taller than I remembered.

'There was no one here,' I said. 'It's strange, this open shop.'

'The only thing to do is to help yourself to the dog and a rose,' he said.

And he picked a rose from a vase and presented it to me. The dog, instead of showing disapproval of this piece of larceny, wagged his tail. Nevertheless we left him at his post and went out into the sunshine. Louis Dalet was still holding my hand and nothing seemed more natural. We walked down the boulevard du Montparnasse.

'I love this part of Paris,' he said. 'It's one of the few places where you can still see women buying flowers from dogs.'

'I thought you were in the country. Didier told me you were a vet.'

'I come to Paris from time to time, to see my brother. Shall we sit down?'

And without waiting for a reply, he ushered me to a little table on a café terrace. He put my hand back in my lap and took a packet of cigarettes from his pocket. I found the ease of his gestures very attractive.

'Speaking of Didier,' he said, 'I've only just arrived and haven't yet seen him. How is he?'

'I've only spoken to him on the telephone. I only got back a couple of days ago myself.'

'Where have you been?'

'In New York and then Nassau.'

For a moment I was afraid that he would talk about Julius with the same bitterness as at our first meeting, but he refrained. He seemed carefree, happy and relaxed, and looked younger.

'Of course,' he said, 'that's why you're so brown.'

And he turned towards me and inspected me. He had astonishingly light-coloured eyes.

'Was it the trip of your dreams?'

'I went to see my husband, who's ill . . .'

I stopped. Suddenly the New York clinic, the absurdly white beach, the image of the unconscious Julius and the absurdly handsome pianist – suddenly it all seemed like part of an old film, in technicolor and somehow over-exposed. All I could see in their true colours were the face of the man beside me, the grey pavement and the trees peacefully blossoming as far as the corner of the street. For the first time since my return, I felt that I was back home. Everything had been so muddled for the past few days. Whether it was Julius's speech in the aeroplane, begging me to forget his momentary aberration in Nassau, whether it was my boss Ducreux's oddly enthusiastic welcome, whether it was Didier's relieved voice on the telephone, doubt and confusion had been the principal colours in my life. I had taken refuge in the status quo suggested by Julius, but the past few weeks had left me with an impression of messiness and sadness until the moment when the basset hound and Louis Dalet had simultaneously entered my life.

'I wish I had a dog,' I said.

'I have a friend in Versailles,' said Louis Dalet, 'whose bitch has just had a litter. They're charming little puppies. I'll get one for you.'

'What sort of dog?'

He laughed.

'Weird, half alsatian, half labrador. You'll see tomorrow. I'll bring it to your office . . .'

I began to be seriously alarmed.

'But they have to be inoculated, and . . .'

'Yes, yes, of course. I'm a vet, remember.'

Then he gave me a hilarious account of all the catastrophes I might expect in my new life as dog owner, and I giggled with fright. The time passed much too quickly. It was after seven o'clock and I was to dine with the dreaded Mme Debout, a prospect which seemed more deadly boring than ever. I would gladly have spent the evening sitting there talking about dogs and cats and goats and watching the night descend over the town. Instead, I had to face that gossipy little gang, no doubt agog at the idea of Julius and me having had a honeymoon on the idyllic island of Nassau. I shook hands with my vet and regretfully dashed off. At the corner of the street I turned round and saw him still sitting there with his head tilted slightly backwards, gazing at the trees.

Julius was waiting for me in my little sitting room and I hastily changed and did my face in the bathroom. I took care that the door was closed. With anyone else, I would have left it ajar in order to talk, but Julius's recent remarks and his proposal of marriage were making me behave like an outraged virgin. The complete absence of danger made everything seem dangerous. And even more annoyingly, since I wasn't out to please the man waiting for me, I wasn't at all pleased by my own reflection in the mirror. So I was not in the happiest of moods when I entered Irène Debout's drawing room. She sailed up to us and went into raptures over how well I looked, but expressed concern at Julius's pallor, the implication being that he was getting too old for amorous escapades in remote islands. All this was doubtless no more than insinuation on her part or imagination on mine, but it immediately irritated me. First I was a kept women, now I was a vampire. It was a more exciting role, perhaps, but I disliked it nonetheless. I glanced round the room and recognized several faces which seemed to me to have curiosity and irony written all over them. No doubt about it, I was getting paranoid. To make matters worse, Irène Debout, catching my eye, hastened to tell me that 'Alas, dear Didier would not be with us, because he had a family dinner'. I had a momentary vision of the two young men, Didier and Louis, strolling around the streets of Paris, glad to be together, free to do what they liked with their evening, and I envied them fiercely. What on earth was I doing among these soured old fogies? Actually, as far as that went, I was exaggerating. The average age was not so high, nor the sentiments so low. On the contrary, a general air of satisfaction hovered over the gathering. For if the prospect of entertaining Irène Debout in your own home was already ambitious enough, that of being her guest was doubly so. There was a powerful distinction there that did not go unremarked. Some Parisian households, that evening, must have been very downcast or very angry. All the same, I couldn't help admiring Mme Debout's choice because it was so completely arbitrary: some of her regulars had been left out, some of her rivals invited, some celebrities snubbed, some nonentities included. Unable to fathom the reason for being in favour or disfavour, they would all be doubly impressed: implacably, Irène Debout had let her royal pleasure be known and thus affirmed her absolute sovereignty. She must have sensed it, furthermore, for she was livelier, more talkative than ever, as it were mollified by the success of her maliciousness. And when a rash young woman was foolish enough to ask her whether the so-and-so's were expected, Irène Debout replied with a 'Certainly not!' that was rapped out with the finality of a guillotine. And that 'Certainly not!' although it was a mere show of force on her part, was enough to strike the name of the so-and-so's from many an invitation list that season.

All this I noticed as I glanced round the room, but without my usual zest. When various people complimented me on my tan, I smiled and felt I was getting old. I remembered coming back from summer holidays when I was younger, and the laughing and teasing with which I would compare my face and arms with those of boys and girls of my own age. In those days I was such a keen sun-worshipper that, more often than not, I would emerge victorious. But tonight, if I was indisputably the winner, it was without the slightest sense of triumph. I wasn't back from playing tennis or volley-ball at Arcachon or Hendaye; I was back from a hammock paid for by a rich admirer on a private beach in Nassau. I hadn't acquired my tan through running, diving and physical prowess, but through lassitude and idleness. My body had exerted itself only once, and that had been in the dark, with a handsome pianist. Ah, yes, I was growing old, and at this rate, in a few years' time I would buy myself one of those home exercise machines and would pedal away every day for half an hour or an hour, climbing imaginary hills, but always straining every nerve, hopelessly pursuing the memories of my irresponsible youth. I had such a comic vision of myself perched on that exercise bicycle that I almost laughed aloud. The blessings of self-mockery . . . Why didn't all these people, so stolidly ensconced in their settees, why didn't they laugh at themselves, and at those settees, and at their pleasure in occupying them, and at their hostess, and at their lives and mine? My companion, who was singing the praises of his favourite corner of the Caribbean, fell silent and looked at me reproachfully.

'Why are you laughing?'

'Why aren't *you* laughing?' I answered brusquely.

'I wasn't saying anything particularly funny . . .'

God knows that was true, but I refrained from pointing it out to him. I had never found gratuitous rudeness amusing. The doors of the dining room opened and we went in to dinner. I found myself next to Julius who in turn was next to Irène Debout.

'I didn't want to separate you,' she said in her famous *mezza voce* which, as usual, made a dozen people jump, and for a second I despised her so intensely that her famous frank stare wavered beneath mine. She averted her eyes and smiled to herself, something she never did. I knew that this smile was intended for me and that it meant: 'You hate me, and I'm delighted: let battle commence.' When she turned to me again with an innocent, abstracted look I smiled back at her and bowed my head in a silent toast that she didn't understand. Because what I was thinking was simply: 'Good-bye, you won't be seeing me again. You and your friends are too boring. I'm just bored, and for me that's worse than hate.' Actually, I was almost sad about this farewell because, in a way, her manic drive, her love of persecuting people, her quickness and her cunning, all the deadly weapons she wielded for such petty ends, made her at once pitiful and fascinating to watch.

The dinner seemed endless. Back in the drawing room, I wandered over to a window and inhaled the cold, acrid night air, that relentlessly desolate breeze that prowled through the city, sweeping over the sleeping population and ruffling the night-owls and bringing dreams of the countryside to all those heads heavy with sleep or alcohol. And for me, in this stiff drawing room dedicated to out-worn airs and graces, that fierce, primeval wind, sweeping down from some remote galaxy, was my only friend, the only tangible proof of my existence. When it died down and my hair settled once more on my brow, I felt as though my very heart were sinking and that I must die. And why not die? I lived because I had no choice, because a man and a woman had loved each other thirty years before. Why should I not choose to die because thirty years later a woman – to wit, myself – didn't love anyone and consequently had no desire to bring another life into the world? The most elementary and the most flatly logical arguments are often the best. One had only to see the degree of chaos to which a society inundated with pseudo-science, pseudo-morality and pseudo-wisdom had been reduced. When you thought about it, when you listened to it, thousands of voices, terrified, yearning, anguished voices, were borne upon that night wind, voices both very distant and very close, living voices frozen by their sheer profusion and monotony into the hollow silence of a huge iceberg – or a referendum. My mind wandered along these lines, without apparent ill-effect: I smiled, nodded my thanks for a light, and put in an occasional remark at all the right moments, trivial in itself but relevant to the conversation. I felt remote from them all. But not, alas, superior. And my remoteness made me more doubtful of my ability to comprehend these people than of the people themselves. In the name of who or what was I to judge them? And if, that night, I felt an urgent need to escape, to get away from them, I should have been quite incapable of explaining why, unless it was a kind of moral asthma, a kind of suffocation for which they were no more responsible than I was. True, their rules of precedence, of success or failure, were beyond my comprehension and I hadn't the least desire to learn them. I had to break away and kick for touch, to use a rugby term: having played a fast wing-forward's game throughout my adolescence and been a tenacious prop in the centre of the scrum with Alan, I was now giving up the game: a cardiac case, I was quitting the green playing field, slightly yellowing now, and without referee or rules, that had been mine. I was alone; I was nothing.

Julius interrupted this flight of fancy. He was at my side, looking glum.

'You found that dinner a bit long-drawn out, didn't you? You seem deep in thought.'

'I was inhaling the night air. I love it.'

'I wonder why.'

He sounded so hostile that I was taken aback.

'At night, you feel that the wind's coming from the country, that it's swept over fresh earth, trees, northern beaches . . . it's comforting . . .'

'It's swept over fields where thousands of corpses are buried, over trees that feed on them, over a dying planet, over beaches polluted by a polluted sea . . . Is that what you call comforting?'

I looked at him, flabbergasted. I had never credited

him with the slightest degree of lyricism, and if I had, it would have been of a conventional kind: alpine glaciers, edelweiss, the purity of nature. Morbid sentiments were something I found incompatible with a businessman's efficiency. Clearly my thought processes were too stereotyped and elementary. He looked at me and smiled.

'I tell you this planet is sick. And this drawing room you despise so much is merely a small abscess in the process of decay. And one of the least of them, I assure you.'

'You *are* cheerful,' I murmured, rather bewildered.

'No, I'm not,' he said. 'I've never been cheerful.'

And he went off, leaving me on my sofa. I watched him cross the room, his glasses glinting in the lights, his slight torso straight as a ramrod. He no longer bore the smallest resemblance to the Julius A. Cram of Nassau, the one who had lain crumpled on the beach in his navy-blue blazer and had complained of neglect from the depths of a vast hammock. No, here in this drawing room, swift and cold and more contemptuous by far than I could ever be, he was frightening. And when, as usual, people withdrew a little as he passed by, for once I understood why.

The next afternoon, about five o'clock, I was told that a man and a dog were waiting for me in the front office of the magazine. I hurried down. And there indeed they were, man and dog, the one carrying the other, silhouetted against the daylight, or rather the sunlight, behind the big glass doors. I went to greet them and was instantly caught up in a whirlwind of hairs and little yelps. I clung to Louis and for a moment we must have looked the very picture of a united family meeting on a station platform. The dog, which was black and tan with huge paws, covered me with kisses as if it had been waiting for two months – all its life – to meet me. Louis smiled and I was so delighted, so overcome suddenly, that I kissed him too. The dog began barking furiously and the entire staff of the magazine left their offices to come and look at him. After a deluge of 'Isn't he sweet? Look at those big paws! He's going to be enormous,' etc., and an undignified tussle with the dog beneath the desk of an astonished Ducreux, Louis took things in hand.

'We must buy him a collar and lead. Plus a bowl and a basket. And then we must decide on a name. Come on.'

These plans seemed to be a good deal more urgent than the vague article I had been struggling with since lunch, so we set off, Louis holding the puppy under his arm and me by the hand. It was clear from his determined stride that we had no choice but to follow him. He had a grey Peugeot outside and we clambered in. Louis planted the dog in my lap and, before driving off, glanced at me triumphantly.

'Well then,' he said, 'I suppose you thought I wouldn't come. You seemed surprised to see me.'

In fact, I hadn't been surprised at seeing him so much as at the sudden happiness I had felt. Catching sight of him with the dog against the window, I had had the curious sensation of suddenly finding my family. But I kept this to myself.

'No, I was sure that you'd come. You're not the sort of man who makes promises he doesn't intend to keep.'

'What a psychologist you are!'

We crossed half the town to find the shop he wanted. Paris was blue, mild, purring; the dog covered me with hairs; I was blissfully content. We let him out for a moment on the Esplanade des Invalides. He chased the pigeons, wrapped his lead round my legs half a dozen times, and seemed to be overflowing with energy. I was torn between laughter and alarm. What on earth would I do with him all day? Louis looked at me mockingly, clearly amused at my onset of panic.

'Ah, yes,' he said, 'you've taken on a real responsibility at last. He'll be dependent on you. That'll be a change for you, won't it?'

I looked at him suspiciously. I didn't know whether he was referring to Julius, to my hunted existence, or to my tendency to run away. We went back home. I introduced the puppy to the concierge who looked anything but pleased, and we sat in my room while the animal proceeded to chew the rug.

'What were you going to do this evening?' Louis asked.

That imperfect was disquieting. In fact, I was going to a private showing of a film with Julius and Didier. I could no more see myself taking the dog than leaving it behind alone. Louis at once anticipated the latter possibility.

'If you leave him alone, he'll howl,' he said. 'And come to that, so will I.'

'You?'

'Yes, if you abandon us both this evening, he'll bark his head off and instead of calming him down I'll join in. Then, tomorrow, you'll be kicked out of the flat.'

'Have you a better idea?'

'Much better. I'll go and do some shopping. Since the weather's mild, we'll open the window and we'll all three dine here quietly, so that the puppy and I can accustom ourselves to your new life.'

He was joking, of course, but he seemed very determined. I prevaricated.

'I'll have to telephone,' I said. 'What I'm doing is very bad manners.'

In so saying, I was admitting that I too couldn't imagine a better way of spending the evening than the one he had just described. I must have looked sheepish, because he burst out laughing and got to his feet.

'That's right, you telephone and I'll go and buy enough Chum for three.'

He disappeared. I sat there in a daze for a moment, then the puppy ran up to me, clambered on to my lap, and began to chew my hair. For the next ten minutes, I gazed at him, talked to him, told him how charming, beautiful and clever he was, like a besotted idiot. I had to make my telephone call before Louis came back. Julius's dry, clipped voice came on the line, and for the first time since I had met him, the sound of that voice was embarrassing rather than comforting.

'Julius, I'm terribly sorry, but I can't come this evening.'

'Are you ill?'

'No,' I said, 'I've got a dog.'

There was a moment's silence.

'A dog? Who gave you a dog?'

I was taken aback. After all, I might easily have bought myself a dog, or found one. Julius seemed to assume that all my acquisitions must be presents. No doubt he thought me totally lacking in initiative, and in this particular instance he was right.

'It was Didier's brother,' I said. 'Louis Dalet. He brought a dog round to me at the magazine.'

'Louis Dalet?' said Julius. 'The vet? Do you know him?'

'A little,' I said in a vague tone of voice. 'Anyway, I've now got this dog, and I can't leave him tonight because they'll howl . . . he'll howl,' I corrected myself.

'But that's absurd,' Julius said. 'Would you like me to send Mlle Barot to cope with it?'

'Your secretary's not going to look after my dog. In any case, he needs to get to know me.'

'Listen,' Julius said, 'I don't understand any of this. I'll be round in an hour.'

'Oh no,' I said, 'don't . . .'

I tried desperately to think up some excuse. Nothing seemed to me more calculated to ruin the evening than the appearance of Julius, all business-like efficiency. The puppy would be dispatched to a dogs' home, in some smart suburb, no doubt, I would be dragged to the cinema with Julius, and as for Louis, I was sure that he'd return to the country and I'd never see him again. And the thought of that, I realized, was unbearable.

'No,' I said, 'I'm going to take him for a walk, buy him a few things. In fact, I'm just on the way out.'

There was a silence.

'What sort of dog is it?'

'I don't know, he's black and tan. It's difficult to tell what breed he is.'

'You should have told me you wanted a dog, I know all the best kennels.'

He sounded reproachful. I began to feel irritated.

'Well, it just happened,' I said. 'Julius, forgive me, but the puppy's calling me. I'll see you tomorrow.'

He said 'all right' and hung up. I heaved a sigh of relief, rushed into the bathroom, pulled on a sweater and trousers, a suitable get-up for a dog, and redid my make-up to give myself a suitable face for a man. I put on a record, opened the window, laid three places on the desk and hummed to myself, thoroughly pleased with life. I was free, I had a baby to care for and a seductive stranger to provide for us. It was the first time for a long, long while that I had a date with an unknown man whom I found attractive and who was my own age. Ever since I had known Alan, my rare amorous adventures had been like the one with the pianist in Nassau. Yes, for the first time in five years I had an assignation with someone that made my heart beat faster.

By ten o'clock, the dog was asleep and at last Louis was telling me a little about himself.

'You must have thought me terribly boorish the first time we met,' he said. 'Actually, I was attracted to you the minute I saw you in that bar, and when I realized that you were Josée, the same girl Didier had told me about who went around with that set I can't bear, I was so disappointed, not to say furious, that I made myself thoroughly unpleasant.'

He stopped and suddenly turned towards me.

'In fact, as soon as you walked into that bar and I handed you the paper, I felt that you'd belong to me one day, and to discover five minutes later that you belonged to Julius A. Cram made me wild with jealousy and disappointment.'

'You don't waste time,' I said.

'No, I've always acted on impulse, too much so. When my parents died, leaving us a big furniture business here in Paris, I decided to let Didier look after it. I'd qualified as a vet and I pushed off to the Sologne, where the life suits me better. Didier quite likes Paris, art galleries, private views, and all those people I can't stand.'

'What have you got against them?'

'Nothing I can put my finger on. They're more dead than alive. They only live for money and appearances, and in my view they're dangerous. Mixing with them makes you feel trapped and sad.'

'There's no need to feel trapped unless you're dependent on them,' I said.

'You're always dependent on the people you live with. That's why I was so horrified to learn that you were involved with Julius A. Cram. He's as cold as ice as well as raving mad . . .'

I stopped him.

'First of all, I'm not involved with Julius A. Cram.'

'I believe that now,' he said.

'Furthermore,' I added, 'he's always behaved impeccably towards me – he's been very kind and completely disinterested.'

'Anyone would think you were twelve years old,' he said. 'God knows how I shall ever be able to make you understand the danger you're in. But I will in time.'

He put out his hand and pulled me towards him. My heart pounded with a noise like thunder. He took me in his arms and held me still for a moment, his cheek against my forehead, and I could feel that he was trembling. Then he kissed me. And the myriad bugles of desire rang out, the myriad tom-toms of the blood throbbed in our veins, and the myriad violins of sensual pleasure struck up their waltz for us. Later, in the dark, lying in each other's arms, we whispered delirious words, we lamented not having met twenty years sooner and we asked each other how we had managed to live up till then. The dog slept on beneath the table, as innocent as we ourselves now were.

I loved him. I didn't know why, why him, why so quickly, why so violently, but I loved him. One night together had been enough to make my life seem like that famous round, ripe apple and to make me feel, once he had left, as if I were only half the apple, freshly severed, vulnerable to everything that came from him and to nothing else. All at once I had swung from the realm of solitude to the realm of love and I could hardly believe that I had the same features, the same name, the same age. I had never been quite sure who I was, objectively speaking, but now I had no idea at all. I only knew that I was in love with Louis and I was amazed that it wasn't immediately apparent to everyone I met. I was once again inhabited by a creature who was warm, alive, triumphant – myself – and my steps had a direction, my words a meaning, my breath a purpose. When I thought about him, which was continually, I wanted to make love to him, and it was in anticipation of this that I gave my body food and drink, since my body pleased him. And dates and days of the week once more had names and numbers, since he had left on Tuesday the nineteenth and was coming back on Saturday the twenty-third. It mattered, too, that the weather should be fine, because then the roads would be dry and his car wouldn't be in danger of skidding, just as it mattered that the lines between Paris and the Sologne should remain free, that there should be telephones everywhere I went and that his voice should emerge from each one, calm, urgent or anxious, his voice happy or full of longing, simply his voice. Nothing else mattered, except the dog, orphaned like me but seemingly better able to bear it.

Julius A. Cram was still perplexed by the dog. To establish its origins would, he said, require a prolonged inquiry by a private detective. Nevertheless, the dog having torn his tweed trousers as a sign of affection, he seemed to warm towards it. And since we were to dine in a quiet restaurant with Didier and a few hangers-on, he decided to invite it too. Or so I let him believe, for I'd made up my mind to bring it anyway. I found Julius divine, the hangers-on witty, the food delicious. As for Didier, it was enough that he was his brother's brother. All that mattered was that I should be back home by half past eleven because Louis was to telephone me at midnight and I wanted to be in bed, in what I termed 'his place', ready to talk to him in the dark for as long as he wanted.

'That was an odd notion of your brother's,' Julius said to Didier, pointing to the dog. 'I had no idea they knew each other, he and Josée.'

'We all had a drink together about a month ago,' Didier said.

He seemed ill at ease.

'And he promised you a dog there and then?'

Julius smiled at me, and I smiled back.

'No. Actually, I ran into him in the street the other day, in a florist's shop, in fact, where there was a dog but no florist, and while I was talking about the flowers to the dog, Louis came in and said I should help myself to a rose and the dog and . . .'

'So the dog belonged to the florist?' Julius asked.

'No, no, of course not,' I said crossly.

They both looked at me in bewilderment. To them, the story must have sounded extremely involved, whereas for me it seemed as clear as daylight. I had seen Louis, he had given me a dog and I loved him. All the rest was immaterial. I had a man with dark hair and brown eyes and a black and tan dog with black eyes. I shrugged my shoulders and they seemed content to leave the mystery unsolved.

'Is your brother as much of a country bumpkin as ever?' Julius asked Didier. Then, turning to me: 'I used to know him slightly, he's a nice chap. But what an odd thing to do, to turn his back on a ready-made job in Paris ... And, by the way, what happened to his girl friend, Barbara?'

'I don't think they see each other any more,' Didier said.

'Barbara Crift, the film producer's daughter,' Julius explained for my benefit. 'She was madly in love with Louis Dalet and wanted to follow him to the country. I imagine she soon got bored with the life of a country vet.'

I smiled pityingly. But not in the way he supposed. In my opinion, this Barbara woman had been out of her mind to leave Louis, and must be bored by now, Paris or no Paris.

'It was Louis who left her,' Didier pointed out with the pride of a younger brother.

'Naturally, naturally,' said Julius. 'The whole of Paris knows that your brother is irresistible to women.'

He gave a sceptical little laugh and looked at me with benign amusement.

'I trust you're not going to follow their example, my dear Josée. But I doubt it: somehow I can't see you in the country.'

'I've never lived there,' I said. 'I only know towns and beaches.'

And as I spoke, I saw stretching out before me acre upon acre of plough, woods, grass and corn. I saw the two of us, Louis and me, walking between two rows of trees while the wind blew the smoke from a bonfire of dead leaves into our faces, and I felt as though, unconsciously, I had always dreamed of living in the country.

'Well, you're about to find out what it's like,' Julius said. I gave a start.

'You haven't forgotten that we're all going to spend the weekend with the Aprenans? Will you be there, Didier?'

The weekend . . . he must be out of his mind. I had completely forgotten the Aprenans' invitation. They were an amiable couple, great friends of Irène Debout, who, having exiled themselves far from Paris out of a grotesque affectation for the simple life, spent their time when they came to the capital, roughly a hundred times a year, extolling the charms of solitude. They lived for their weekend house parties. The only trouble was that Louis was arriving on Saturday, and we were to spend two whole days alone together in my flat. Saturday seemed to me so near and so far away that I felt like dancing for joy and bewailing my fate at one and the same time. I knew that Louis had very broad shoulders and an impressive scar on his arm (a donkey had bitten him while he was treating it, a story that had made us laugh for a good ten minutes), I knew that he cut himself shaving and that he put his shoes on last when he dressed. That was about all I knew about him apart, of course, from the fact that I loved him. I thought of all the things I still had to discover about his body and his past and his character, and felt dizzy with curiosity, hunger and tenderness. Meanwhile I had to find some excuse about the weekend. The easiest thing, of course, would have been to say: 'Look, I'm spending those two days with Louis Dalet, because that's what I want to do', but I couldn't bring myself to do so. I felt guilty once again and it made me furious with myself. After all, Julius had spoken to me of his feelings following an attack of sunstroke, he hadn't wanted an answer, and the straightforward, honest thing to do would have been to tell him the truth. Objectively, yes, except that beneath the clear, unruffled surface of the obvious, there lay all the monstrous, hidden shadows of a secret truth. Not for the first time, I was irritably conscious of the inanity of such words as 'objectively', 'clear-cut situation', 'independence', 'friendship', etc., and, above all, I felt that in confessing to Julius – and already I was thinking in terms of 'confessing' rather than 'telling' – I might provoke an excess of anger, bitterness and vengefulness that terrified me. The kind of black halo that surrounded this man, the atmosphere of power and tension he created, in the long run never failed to frighten me. And yet, what could he do to me? I had a job; I was in no way dependent on him; I only risked hurting him. And if this last feeling was strong enough to make me feel uncomfortable, it still shouldn't have been strong enough to enforce the silence and the half-truths I had automatically been observing for the past three days. To the extent that my life had been transformed into a sort of sunlit open road of passion, I could hardly bear for anything to cast the least shadow across it.

All these problems vanished at midnight when I heard Louis's voice asking me if I loved him, in that tone of his that was at once incredulous and triumphant. He said 'Do you love me?' as if to say 'I can't believe you love me, I know you love me, why do you love me? How could you not love me? I love you . . .' I should have liked to ask him where he was, I should have liked him to describe his bedroom, what he could see out of his window, what he had done that day, but the words wouldn't come. No doubt I would ask him later on, when his presence had acquired that other dimension, mellower, less intense, that memory confers, but for the moment I knew him as the man of a single night, I had seen him more in darkness than in daylight, he was for me a body burning with desire, a head thrown back, a silhouette at dawn, he was warmth, a look or two, a weight, half a dozen sentences. Beyond all else, he was a lover. But I couldn't remember the way he drove or how he stubbed his cigarettes out in an ashtray. Or how he slept, since we hadn't slept. On the other hand, I knew his face and his voice in the act of love. And in that domain too, the vast domain of sensual pleasure, I knew that we had a thousand discoveries to make together, a thousand acres of countryside to explore, lying side by side, a thousand meadows to cavort in, a thousand fires to extinguish, fires that we ourselves had started. I knew that we would be insatiable, he and I, and I couldn't imagine, inexorable though it must be, the day when that mutual hunger would subside. And he had said Saturday and I had repeated Saturday, as two castaways might say 'land' or two damned souls, wonderstruck, might apostrophize hell. And he arrived on Saturday at midday and left on Monday morning, and it was both heaven and hell. One or other of us took the dog out two or three times and those were the only moments when we saw daylight. I discovered that he preferred Mozart to Beethoven, that he had fallen off his bicycle several times as a child, and that he slept on his stomach. I discovered he was funny and occasionally sad. I discovered he was tender. The telephone rang a dozen times, insistently, during those two days, and I let it ring. When he left me, I leant against him, tottering a little from exhaustion and happiness and I implored him to drive carefully.

'I promise,' he said. 'You know quite well that I can't die now.'

'One of these days,' he added, 'I'll buy a great big car, as slow and sure as a bus. An old Daimler, for instance, like the one that's always parked beneath your window at night.'

On Friday, my courage failing me as usual, I had sent a highly elliptical telegram to Julius at his office: 'Impossible come weekend stop explanation follows stop many apologies Josée.' Now all I had to do was to invent the excuse. My mind had been a blank when I sent the telegram, Louis's arrival being imminent and my happiness being such as to deprive me of inspiration. Now that this happiness was confirmed, redoubled, I found myself even more devoid of ideas. The presence of the Daimler – assuming it belonged to Julius – parked there for the purpose of spying on me, as it had been for so long beneath Alan's windows, didn't worry me. The chauffeur, assuming there was a chauffeur, would merely be able to report that he had seen me walking a black and tan dog, then that he had seen the same dog being walked by a strange man. I therefore decided to tell Julius that I had to go and see some old friends not far from Paris: either he would believe me or he would know that I was lying, in which case he could embark on one of the cross-examinations he was so good at. It would end in a scene or in recriminations, and a showdown would be a relief to everyone, in particular to me. In other words, I preferred to be convicted of lying than to tell the plain, unvarnished truth. I was getting ready to go out when the telephone rang. It was a call from New York. The next minute I heard my mother-in-law's voice, nasal and domineering, and for a moment I wondered what new ploy Alan had thought up.

'Josée,' said my mother-in-law, 'I'm ringing you about your divorce. Naturally, Alan is determined to do the right thing by you, and so of course am I, but your lawyer seems to be peculiarly recalcitrant. Don't you want a divorce any more?'

'But of course I do,' I said, aghast. 'Why?'

'Dupont-Cormeil, Mr Cram's lawyer, has agreed to everything, including the alimony, but he still hasn't sent us the necessary papers. After all, Josée, you must need some money. At any rate,' she added hurriedly, 'even if you don't need any, it's always nice to have.'

'I really haven't the faintest idea what's going on,' I said. 'I'll find out.'

'Good, please do. And should you ever have dealings with people who may not be as fair and honest as we are, change your lawyer. He appears to think it almost indecent that we want to settle some money on you. A thousand dollars a month is nothing out of the way.'

It was to me. I thanked her absently, promised to look into the whole thing, and hung up, intrigued and above all amazed that Julius's lawyer, who should by rights be a formidable shark, should behave like a lamb when confronted with my no less formidable mother-in-law. Then I forgot all about it.

I was thankful to find a taxi prepared to take myself and the dog because, the buses and the Metro being denied us, my only means of getting to work was either an understanding taxi-driver or my own feet. And to walk, on that particular morning, would have worn me out: I should have felt as though I were dragging along an awkward, clumsy puppy on one lead, and on another, invisible lead, the memory of Louis and of those two days – an even more clumsy and stubborn mastiff than my charming mongrel. Ducreux was waiting for me, or rather his secretary was; she intercepted me on my way in and took me straight into the editor's office. Ducreux was a grey man whose suits, hair and eyes were all uniformly grey, but today he had a pleased, excited air that was infectious. He was a shy, courteous man, devoted to the magazine which he had kept going by the skin of his teeth for the past eight years and which I knew to be a source of considerable financial worry to him.

'My dear Josée,' he said, 'I've got some marvellous news for you. Unless, of course, you know it already. There is a prospect of increasing the size of the magazine from thirty-two to sixty-four pages, changing the format, widening its scope, in other words of turning it into something more than a specialist review.'

'How wonderful,' I said sincerely, for I really liked the magazine both for its seriousness and for its liberal approach and because, little by little, I had come to feel accepted by the staff.

'If it comes off,' Ducreux went on, 'I shall offer you a more important job which will also carry greater responsibility. Partly because I think very highly of you and partly because it's thanks to you that at last I shall be able to do what I've always wanted to do with my magazine.'

'What do you mean? I don't understand,' I said.

He looked at me doubtfully for a minute, then smiled.

'I don't believe you do,' he said. 'In that case you'll be doubly pleased, since it's a great friend of yours, Julius A. Cram, who has offered to back us.'

I sat there nonplussed, then I jumped to my feet, rushed up to Ducreux and kissed him on the forehead. I quickly apologized but he too was smiling with delight.

'It's too good to be true,' I said. 'I'm so pleased for you, and for the others, and for myself. What fun it'll be!

How marvellous of Julius. There's no doubt about it,' I added in my usual unthinking way, 'good things really do all come at once.'

He gave me a quizzical glance but I evaded all explanations with a wave of the hand.

'How long have you known this?' I asked.

'Since this morning. I'd already met Julius A. Cram, of course' – he too gave a wave of his hand that precluded any explanation of that 'of course' – 'but this morning he rang me up and explained to me that he would find it enjoyable and instructive to have an interest in a publication such as ours. At the same time he asked me, with the utmost tact I may say, if I could see my way to involving you more closely with the paper. Had there been the slightest hint of an obligation in what he said, or rather if I hadn't known that you really enjoyed what you were doing, I would have refused, but luckily that didn't arise. Josée, my dear, I'm going to put you in charge of the entire painting and sculpture section together with Max, and I feel sure that you'll be able to devote yourself to it wholeheartedly at last, not to mention having a bit more money.'

'I'm thrilled,' I said.

And I really was. It proved that the early-morning Daimler wasn't the right one, or rather the wrong one; it proved that Julius was beginning to take me seriously as a journalist, in other words as an independent woman; and it also proved that Ducreux, whom I knew to be difficult to please, appreciated my work. Not only had my heart begun to beat again, but my brain too would now begin to function.

'So you have no objection, then?' said Ducreux.

I raised my eyebrows.

'Why should I have?'

'I wanted to be sure,' he said. 'I should also like to say

that if for some reason which is none of my business you were tempted to refuse the job, it would in no way alter our relationship.'

I hadn't the least idea what he was talking about. He must be one of that host of poor fools who believed that hidden links existed between Julius and me, that host of blind deaf-mutes who were unaware of Louis's existence.

'There's no problem of that kind,' I said, with the smugness of requited love. 'What we should be doing is opening a bottle of champagne.'

And ten minutes later eight intellectuals, of whom I counted myself as one, two secretaries and a dog invaded the neighbouring bar and drank the health of the great new magazine to come in three bottles of champagne. Bombarded by questions as to the identity of our miraculous benefactor, Ducreux smiled, murmured about a friend of his and flashed me an occasional slightly quizzical glance which, encouraged by the champagne and my obvious delight, quickly became warm and friendly. I telephoned Didier and insisted that he drop everything and join me for lunch at Charpentier's.

'No,' said Didier, 'no, I can't believe it! I'm absolutely delighted.'

I had just told him of my love for Louis and his for me, and he seemed as happy as he was amazed.

'Louis wanted us to tell you together,' I said, 'but a week without being able to talk about him to anyone seemed to me so long that in the end he gave me permission to tell you.'

'When I think,' Didier said, 'when I think how furious he was with you that first time, and you with him . . .'

'He thought I was Julius's mistress,' I said gaily. 'He didn't like the idea.'

'I told him it wasn't true,' Didier continued, 'but he

said I was a fool. I must admit it was difficult to believe, or rather not to believe. And what about Julius? Does he know?'

'No, not yet, but I'll tell him sooner or later,'

'He didn't seem too pleased at the Aprenans',' Didier went on. 'In fact he seemed furious.'

'Oh no, not at all,' I said. 'Not only is he not furious but he telephoned Ducreux, my nice editor, this very morning and offered to subsidize the magazine. He's suddenly decided it would be fun to lose a bit of money. Isn't it wonderful? Dear Julius . . .'

I felt positively sentimental about him.

'Dear Julius,' Didier repeated thoughtfully. 'It's the first time I've heard of Julius A. Cram taking an interest in a loss-making enterprise.'

He seemed suddenly downcast, and thoughtfully mashed up a potato on his plate.

'You don't suppose,' he said, 'that it's Julius's way of trying to keep a hold on you?'

'No, he wouldn't sink so low as that. In any case Ducreux assured me that didn't enter into it as far as he was concerned and that he appreciated my work. Didier, my dear brother-in-law, do you realize – I love Louis and I've found a career!'

He looked up, scrutinized me, and suddenly, with a to-hell-with-it-all gesture, raised his glass and clinked it against mine.

'Here's to you, Josée,' he said, 'to your love and to your job.'

Then we returned to the principal subject of our conversation, namely Louis. I learnt that he was the most exemplary and understanding of brothers, the most sensitive and friendly of allies, the perfect confidant; I learnt that he had always got involved with women who weren't fit to lick his boots; I learnt what I already knew, that we were quite obviously made for one another.

'But how are you going to manage,' Didier put in, 'working in Paris and living in the country?'

'We'll see,' I said. 'We'll find some sort of compromise.'

'I warn you, Louis doesn't like compromises.'

I knew that and was glad of it.

'We'll find a way, we'll find a way,' I said gaily.

The weather was as glorious as ever. I could still feel the fresh sting of Louis's teeth on my neck. The champagne drunk on an empty stomach made everything deliciously hazy and simple. I held Didier's hand across the table. I was brimming over with happiness. In five days' time, on Friday evening, I should be on the train on my way to join Louis in the Sologne. I should get to know his house, his life, his animals, I should be safely away from it all.

That same night, Didier and I dined with Julius, and the evening was a tremendous success. Julius seemed as delighted as I was with his new venture and I promised to make him a millionaire twice over thanks to the magazine. He confided to us that he had long dreamed of having some interest outside stocks and shares. He even asked us to help him to brush up on his culture – in fact he switched extremely gracefully from the role of generous patron to that of grateful illiterate. He was bored, he seemed to be saying, he liked painting, wanted to have a good time with us, enjoy himself and improve his mind all at the same time. He asked me a few vague questions about my weekend. I simply said that I'd had no alternative and to my great surprise he didn't pursue the matter. Even Didier was prepared to admit afterwards that he might have been mistaken and that Julius, rather late in the day and thanks to me, was revealing a disinterested side to his character that he had failed to notice hitherto. The week went by in a flash. Louis telephoned me, I telephoned Louis. At the magazine, we produced one dummy after another. Didier followed me everywhere. In the evening I would tell him and Julius about our latest brainwaves. On the Thursday, the three of us dined with Ducreux, who in his turn seemed overcome by the niceness, the relaxed ease and lack of intellectual pretension of Julius A. Cram. I had intended to tell Julius that evening that I was leaving next day to spend the weekend with Louis Dalet in the country, but the dinner party had been such fun, we had all been so delighted with one another, that I was reluctant to embark on awkward explanations on the way home in his car. I simply told him I was going off to the country with Didier, which happened to be true, since he was coming with me. And he said to me 'I'll see you on Monday, then – don't forget we're dining with Irène Debout,' without the slightest sign of resentment. I watched his slightly balding skull, scarcely visible over the back of the seat, disappearing into the night, and remembering what a comforting image that same bald head had been for me one evening at Orly, I suddenly felt a pang on realizing that it had become instead the very symbol of loneliness.

The train shrieked like a thing possessed and shook us in rhythm with its frenzied motion, but I felt sure it was at a standstill and that on either side of the carriage railwaymen were rushing past, heads down, carrying trees, in order to give us a false impression of speed. We had changed trains en route and I who had always been so fond of old-fashioned country trains found myself longing for one of those thundering, inhuman expresses which would have brought me more quickly to my goal: Louis. After having done his best to interest me in crossword puzzles, gin rummy and the latest political gossip, Didier had resigned himself to travelling with a ghost and dipped into a detective story. From time to time he glanced at me mockingly and hummed *La Vie en Rose*. It was seven in the evening, the shadows were lengthening, the countryside looked beautiful.

At long last our carriage came to a halt at Louis's feet and decanted me into his arms. Didier got down the luggage and the dog and we all climbed into the open Peugeot. Before driving off, Louis turned towards us and we all three gazed at one another and smiled. I knew it was a moment I should never forget: the little deserted station at sunset, those two faces, so alike and yet so different, turned towards me, the country smell, the silence after the noise of the train, the happiness that pierced me like an exquisite dagger-thrust. For a second everything stood still, everything photographed itself for ever on the sensitized plate of my memory, then Louis's hands returned to the wheel and we came to life once more.

A country road, a village, a rough track, and we were at the house: square and low, its windows blinded by the yellow glint of the sun, an ancient tree dozing in front of it, two dogs. My dog immediately woke up from its deep puppy sleep and rushed up to them, barking. I was panic-stricken but the two men shrugged their shoulders, slammed the car doors and climbed the short flight of steps into the house, suitcases in hand, with the vigorous, placid movements of countrymen. In the sitting room there was a big velvet sofa, a piano, some potted ferns, newspapers everywhere and an enormous fireplace that I fell in love with there and then, though I should have been just as happy with Gothic chairs or abstract designs. I went over to the French windows which opened on to a cottage garden and then an endless field of clover.

'How peaceful it is here,' I said as I turned round.

And Louis crossed the room and put his hand on my shoulder.

'Do you like it?'

I raised my eyes to his. I hadn't dared to look him full in the face until then. I was intimidated by him, by myself, by everything that had passed between us from the moment we were in each other's presence, and which seemed to me almost palpable. His hand was scarcely touching my shoulder: he had placed it there cautiously, hesitantly. His face was slightly tense, and I could hear his breath coming in short gasps. We looked at one another without really seeing, and I felt that my face was as naked as his and that, like his, it was crying out 'it's you', 'it's you', without moving a muscle. Faces ravaged by love, planets of petrified lava, with the soundless, liquid seas of looks exchanged and the chasm of closed lips; the blue veins throbbing at our temples were an indecent anachronism, the stubborn reminder of a time when we thought we existed, loved, slept and yet did not know each other. And I had thought before knowing him that the sun was hot, that silk was soft and that the sea was salt. I had lived in a dream so long, I had even fancied I was growing old, and I had not yet been born.

'I'm famished, I'm famished!' came Didier's voice from miles away, and as it reached us we awoke. Suddenly I noticed that Louis already had a slight sun-tan, with little white lines showing through it below his eyes.

'You must have been reading in the sun,' I said.

And he smiled at last and nodded his head; his hand squeezed my shoulder and he stepped back. Our bodies too had remained motionless until then, a yard apart, stiffly resisting the fierce geotropism of mutual desire; our bodies had remained at a distance from their prey, stock still, like two well-trained pointers. At Louis's step they relaxed, we moved towards one another quite naturally and walked back side by side to Didier. He smiled.

'I hope you don't mind me saying so, but you both look half-witted,' he said. 'And anything but cheerful. Why don't we have a drink ... I'm beginning to feel like a Spanish duenna with an engaged couple.'

Knowing as I did how the awkwardness of daytime can belie the harmony of the night, how a show of aloofness can reveal a secret shamelessness, I felt a sudden access of pride and gratitude vis-à-vis those two violent bodies, Louis's and mine, for their self-mastery in the presence of a third person. Yes, our love had two fine steeds to run its course, two thoroughbreds, mettlesome and true, who liked the wind and the dark. I lay on the sofa, Louis got out a bottle of whisky, Didier put on a Schubert record and we downed our first drink very quickly. I was suddenly overcome with thirst and tiredness. Darkness had fallen; I had been sitting in front of this fireplace for ten years; I could have sung this unfamiliar quintet by heart. Were I to die a hundred deaths, I would sell my soul a hundred times over for such moments in life.

The local restaurant was three hundred yards away and we walked there. It was very dark on the way back, but we could see the road in front of us, pale and white. Louis's bedroom was large and empty. He left both windows open and the night air, wafting from one to the other, breathed on us from time to time, light and solicitous, refreshing us, drying our bodies, compassionate as a slave watching over two of his comrades, themselves the slaves of a more pitiless master.

It was two days later, on the Sunday, that a cow in the neighbourhood decided to calve. Louis suggested that we should accompany him and both Didier and I were equally reluctant.

'Come on,' said Louis, 'for the last two days you've done nothing but rhapsodize over the charms of the countryside, the pair of you. After the flora, the fauna. Let's go.'

We travelled about ten miles at top speed. I tried to remember the passage in a fine novel by Roger Vailland where the heroine, a woman at once tough and fragile, helps to bring a calf into the world. After all, if my life was to be spent between subtle discussions about Impressionism or the Baroque on the one hand and the more earthy caprices of nature on the other, it was essential for me to do some homework.

It was dark inside the stable. A woman, two men and a child were standing around a loose-box from which came the most heartrending cries. A peculiar smell, at once stale and pungent, mixed with that of the manure. I suddenly realized that it was the smell of blood. Louis took off his jacket, rolled up his sleeves, and stepped forward as the two men stood aside, and I saw something grey, pink and viscous which seemed to be an extension of the cow. She groaned a little and the thing seemed to grow bigger. I realized that it was the calf emerging and I rushed outside, overcome with nausea. Didier followed me on the pretext of helping me, but he was shaking all over. We looked at one another pitifully and then burst out laughing. The transition from Mme Debout's drawing room to this farmyard had been rather abrupt, to say the least. The cow uttered another heartrending cry and Didier handed me a cigarette.

'What an awful business!' he said. 'If this is how my dear brother hopes to reconcile me to the idea of fatherhood . . . Personally, I intend to wait out here.'

A little later, we went in to admire the new-born calf; then Louis washed his bloodstained arms, the farmer gave us a glass of home-made alcohol and we returned to the car. Louis laughed.

'That wasn't a very conclusive test,' he said.

'It was for me,' declared Didier. 'I've never experienced anything like it. I don't know how you can do it.'

Louis shrugged his shoulders.

'Actually, that poor cow didn't need me at all. I'm only there in case something should go wrong. Sometimes they need stitching afterwards.'

'Do shut up,' Didier said. 'Think of our delicate stomachs.'

Out of pure sadism, Louis launched into the minutest details, each more horrifying than the last, until we had to put our fingers in our ears. We stopped in the woods, beside a lake. The two men began skimming stones.

'Has Josée told you about Julius A. Cram's latest whim?' asked Didier.

'No,' I said. 'It didn't even occur to me.'

Louis was leaning forward, stone in hand, and he turned to look at me.

'What's that?'

'Julius has decided to finance the magazine Josée works for,' Didier announced. 'This young lady who has just seen a cow calve is to pronounce on the future of contemporary painting and sculpture.'

'Well, well,' said Louis.

Then he flung back his arm and his stone bounced five or six times on the smooth surface of the lake before disappearing.

'Not bad,' he said, pleased with himself. 'That's quite a responsibility, isn't it?'

He looked at me, and suddenly the exhilarating prospect of my new job seemed unreal and full of pitfalls. How could I claim to be able to judge the works of others when my own judgement was so unsure? I must be mad. Louis's expression made me believe I *was* mad.

'Didier is putting it badly,' I said. 'In fact, I shan't really be a critic. I'll simply write about what I admire and what I like.'

'But that's not the reason you're mad,' said Louis. 'Do you realize that you'll be paid, whether you write or don't write, by Julius A. Cram?'

'By Ducreux,' I corrected him.

'Through Ducreux,' Louis went on. 'You can't possibly agree to that.'

I looked at him, I looked at Didier, who had lowered his eyes, no doubt upset at having broached the subject, and I lost my temper. As in the Pont Royal bar, I saw Louis as an enemy, a judge, a puritan, I no longer saw him as my best-beloved.

'I've been doing it for three months,' I said. 'I may lack experience, but it's a living and what's more I find it extremely interesting. I couldn't care less whether I'm paid by Ducreux or Julius.'

'But I care,' said Louis.

He picked up another stone. His face was grim. For a moment I thought stupidly that he was going to throw the stone in my face.

'Everyone believes I'm Julius's mistress,' I said. 'At any rate, everyone believes he keeps me.'

'That must be changed too,' Louis interrupted, 'and quickly.'

What did he expect to change, after all? As a city, Paris wasn't open and above board, and that set lived on nothing but evasions and false pretensions. But I belonged to Louis and to him alone, and he knew it. Did he expect me never to admire anyone else but him? Did he expect me to give up my solitary prowls through the museums, the galleries, the streets of the town? Couldn't he understand that a certain blue in a canvas here, a certain shape there, meant more to me than a new-born calf? Just as I felt myself to be more alive, more real through his eyes, I found nature richer, more dazzling, through the eyes of a painter. Was I degenerate, blue-stocking, pretentious? In any case, there was nothing I could do about it; I was no longer eighteen years old and I wasn't looking for a Pygmalion, whether he was a vet or not. I was brooding over these dark thoughts and staring blankly at the road, when Louis took my hand in his.

'Don't be cross,' he said. 'We've got plenty of time for everything.'

Then he smiled at me and I smiled back, and I would willingly have promised there and then to stay with him for ever and devote myself exclusively to cattle-breeding. My change of mood must have been palpable because Didier, who had been sitting beside me with clenched teeth, suddenly heaved a sigh and began whistling *La Vie en Rose*. That evening, that night, if we had time, if our two bodies in their preoccupation with pleasure, their fear of separation, allowed us the time, we would talk it over. But already, weakly, voluptuously, I knew that neither he nor I would allow anything to come between us and that the only words we uttered would be words of love.

'I can't go to London,' I said. 'I can't possibly leave tomorrow.'

'Listen,' said Julius. 'there's a sale at Sotheby's on Friday, Saturday and Monday. And Ducreux is so keen on your going . . .'

We were sitting on the terrace of Fouquet's and Irène Debout had just joined us.

'Don't you like London?' she asked. 'It's such a beautiful city and Sotheby's sales are very exciting. Take Didier along, if you're afraid of being bored.'

I didn't know what to say. Louis was due to arrive the next day and I couldn't imagine him wanting to come with me. For the past five days we had talked every evening on the telephone about our hide-out in the rue de Bourgogne, the records we would listen to, the shadowy room in which we would pitch our tent for forty-eight hours. He wouldn't want aeroplanes or hotels or pictures; he would want only me.

'I can't understand you,' said Irène Debout.

'Exactly,' I snapped.

She flushed with anger. I was seeing much less of her these days, of her and her cronies. We worked late at the magazine, in an atmosphere of cheerful excitement, and I went home immediately afterwards. I'd prepare some food for the puppy and myself, and after Louis's telephone call, I'd go to bed and sleep like a log. Julius often came and lunched at a restaurant near the magazine. He seemed as interested in our plans as we were, these days, and like a willing pupil even carried around in his car the albums and art books Ducreux had advised him to buy. And he had insisted on lending me one of his little office runabouts so that I could get around with the dog more easily.

Now, however, I was trapped. I had to give a firm no to the London project and explain my reasons. The presence of Mme Debout, instead of being an embarrassment, made things easier. She would transform my love story into an anecdote, reduce it to a trivial episode, rather tiresome, perhaps, since it involved a professional dereliction, but no more than that. In taxing me with frivolity, she would make my confession more frivolous.

'Didier Dalet won't be able to leave Paris either,' I said. 'We're expecting his brother Louis, who's coming to Paris for a couple of days.'

Julius didn't bat an eyelid but Irène Debout gave a start, stared at me, then turned severely to Julius.

'Louis Dalet?' she said. 'What's all this about, Julius? Do you know what's going on?'

There was a silence that Julius didn't seem anxious to break. He looked down at his hands.

'Julius knows nothing about it,' I said with an effort. 'I haven't known Louis Dalet for long. He's the one who gave me the dog, you know. To cut a long story short, he's coming to Paris this weekend, so I can't go to London.'

Irène Debout burst into strident laughter.

'I've never heard anything so ridiculous,' she said.

'My dear Irène,' Julius began, 'if you don't mind, I'll discuss all this with Josée later on. I don't see much point . . .'

'Neither do I,' she said. 'You can discuss it now, if you want to. I'm off.'

And she got up and left so quickly that Julius barely had time to rise from his chair.

'Well,' I said, 'what's the matter with her?'

'The matter with her,' said Julius, 'is that she thought, as I did too, that you were interested in your job, that it was a real opportunity for you to settle down, and she's a bit disappointed to find that you're prepared to neglect it at the drop of a hat for the sake of a stranger. After all, in spite of her unfortunate manner, Irène is very fond of you and she doesn't realize how quickly you get infatuated.'

'Who are you referring to?' I said.

'I'm referring to Louis Dalet,' said Julius smoothly, 'or for that matter the pianist in Nassau.'

I blushed. I could feel myself blushing.

'How do you know about that?' I said. 'And if you knew, how dare you bring it up! Are you having me watched?'

'I told you that I had your interests at heart.'

His eyes were half-closed behind his glasses, and he wasn't looking at me. I suddenly hated him, hated myself. I rose to my feet so quickly that the dog jumped up and began barking furiously.

'I'm going,' I said. 'I can't bear the idea that . . . that you . . .'

I was stammering with rage and embarrassment. Julius raised his hand with a kindly air.

'Calm down,' he said, 'all that's beside the point. I'll come and pick you up at seven o'clock as arranged.'

But I'd already fled. I strode across the road and jumped into the car with the dog. It wasn't until I was turning on the ignition that I remembered it was 'his' car. However, I couldn't have cared less. At the risk of demolishing his precious machine, I tore down the avenue, across the bridge and back home at top speed. I sat on my bed, my head throbbing, and the dog laid his head in my lap in sympathy. I didn't know what to do with myself.

Five minutes later, Julius rang the doorbell. He sat down opposite me and stared out of the window. Come to think of it, we had never looked one another full in the face. Whenever I thought of him, it was always his profile that I saw. He was an undemonstrative, expressionless man; a man who had seen me when I was Alan's prisoner, in tears in a New York hotel, flirting with a pianist in a bar, a man who could conjure up striking, not to say melodramatic images of me whereas I knew little or nothing about him. The only time he had spoken to me about his innermost feelings, it had been from the depths of a hammock from which only the top of his head was visible. It wasn't a fair fight.

'I know you'd prefer to be left alone,' Julius said, 'but I'd like to explain a few things to you.'

I didn't reply. I looked at him and sincerely wished he would go away. For the first time, I saw him as an enemy. Absurd though it was, my sole preoccupation was this: would he or would he not tell Louis about the pianist? I was perfectly aware that it was a childish reaction with no real bearing on the situation, but I couldn't stop myself thinking about it. Of course it had meant nothing, but I was afraid lest Louis should begin to feel that he too meant nothing; I knew he was temperamental enough to be capable of it.

'The fact is,' Julius said, 'you're angry with me because of the pianist. It wasn't me who saw you that evening, it was Mademoiselle Barot. In any case, you're perfectly free.'

'Do you call that being free?'

'I've always said you must do as you pleased, Josée, and you've always done so. The fact that I'm interested in you and in your life is quite independent of any feelings I may have for you. You think you're in love with Louis, or you *are* in love with him,' he corrected himself, seeing my expression, 'and I find that perfectly natural. But you can't prevent me from worrying about you, and in my own way, watching over you. It's the right and duty of any friend.'

He spoke in a calm, assured voice, and indeed, objectively speaking, what did I have to reproach him with?

'After all,' he went on, 'when we first met you were in a bad way and since then I don't see that I've done anything except try to help you. No doubt I was wrong to unburden myself to you in Nassau, but I was very tired and lonely, and in any case I apologized the next day.'

Yes, this little man, in spite of all his power, was indeed utterly alone whereas I, in my new-found happiness, was behaving with the arrogance and cruelty of the newly rich. I mistrusted him. And for me there had always been something demeaning in mistrust. He continued to look past me, and I got to my feet impulsively and put my hand on his sleeve. After all, he was genuinely fond of me, he was genuinely unhappy and he couldn't help himself.

'Julius,' I said, 'I'm sorry, I really am sorry. I'm very grateful for all that you've done for me. But I felt I was being watched, trapped, and ... And what about the Daimler?' I asked suddenly.

'The Daimler?' said Julius.

'The Daimler parked in the street outside my flat?'

He stared at me, totally mystified. Anyway, I thought, his wasn't the only Daimler in Paris and I didn't even know the colour of the one Louis had seen. Besides, I loathed going into such details. I preferred to keep things on a plane of friendship and affection rather than descend to the tortuous methods of private detection. Yet again, rather than face up to the substance of things, I took refuge in a preoccupation with their form.

'Let's not go into all that,' I said. 'Would you like a drink?'
He smiled.

'Yes, please, and for once something strong.'

He took a little bottle from his pocket, and shook out two pills.

'Are you still taking all those pills?' I asked.

'No more than most people,' he replied.

'Are they tranquillizers? I can't tell you how this mania for pills frightens me.'

It was true. I couldn't understand why people were so desperate to minimize and deaden the varying shocks of life. It seemed to me tantamount to admitting permanent defeat, and this screen interposed between anxiety, unhappiness, boredom and oneself was like a white flag, a sign of surrender, by definition utterly humiliating.

'When you're my age,' Julius said with a smile, 'you won't be able to bear it either, being at the mercy of . . .'

He searched for words.

'At the mercy of someone like me,' I said, with a hint of irony.

He closed his eyes and nodded his head by way of assent, and I no longer had any desire to smile. Perhaps, one day, I too would reach the point of deliberately muzzling the famished wolves of my desires, the screeching birds of my anxieties and regrets. Perhaps, one day, I too would reach the point of being able to tolerate only a sort of carbon copy of myself, black and white, colourless and spineless. Ah yes, the time would come when I would bicycle without ever leaving my bathroom, chewing pills the while to send my feelings to sleep. Muscled legs and flabby heart, a serene face and a dead soul. I had a sudden vision of all this without believing in it, for between this nightmare and myself there was Louis. So I drank a whisky with Julius and we laughed together at the memory of Mme Debout's outraged flight.

'She'll end up by going for me,' I said gaily. 'She doesn't like to be flouted.'

I didn't know how true that was.

Summer had come. In a few more days it would be June. The Luxembourg gardens were welcoming, full of shouting children, exuberant *boule*-players, and a few old ladies perking up in the warmth of the sun. Louis and I were sitting on a bench. We had decided to have a serious talk. As a rule, no sooner were we alone together than his hand or mine would reach out instinctively to the other's hair or face and a kind of beatitude, of purring contentment, would induce us to put off everything except tender gestures until later. Our lives were spent in happy silences and half-finished sentences, as though by tacit consent we had entrusted all meaningful dialogue to our bodies. Nevertheless, today Louis seemed determined to get things straight.

'I've been thinking,' he said. 'First of all, I have a confession to make. Quite apart from my high-minded contempt for social life, I left Paris because I was a gambler, a wild gambler.'

'That's fine,' I said. 'So am I.'

'That's no help. Before running through my entire inheritance, not to mention Didier's, I took myself out of harm's way. I became a vet because I love animals and doctoring dumb creatures is always pleasant. But I don't want to force you to live in the country any more than I want to live without you.'

'I'd come to the country if that's what you wanted,' I said.

'I know you would, but I also know that you love your magazine. And I could just as well work near Paris. I know some people who have a stud farm: I could specialize in racehorses, and that way I need never leave you again.'

I was relieved. I hadn't told Louis that my job, or rather my idea of it, gratified a bizarre desire, new to me, to be good at something. Not only that, I was delighted to discover that Louis was a gambler and that the character of this man, the embodiment of calm and stability ever since I had known him, contained a few flaws. True, the words he whispered at night, his behaviour as a lover revealed an imaginativeness, a sort of gentle wildness that had reassured me. I was aware that night, like alcohol, is a great revealer. But that he should of his own accord admit that he had problems and weaknesses meant that he now had confidence in me, that he had dropped his guard, and that the greatest victory of happy lovers, to be able to lay down their arms, could be ours.

'We'll live near Paris,' Louis said, 'and then, if you like, we'll have a child or two.'

It was certainly the first time in my chequered career that such a possibility had struck me as desirable. I would live in a house with Louis, the dog and the child. I would become the best art critic in Paris. We would breed thoroughbreds in the garden. It would be the happy ending to a tale of storms, pursuit and flight. At last I'd have a change of role: no longer would I be the prey tracked down by a relentless hunter, I'd be the deep, familiar forest where docile, well-loved creatures, my companion, my child and my animals would come for shelter, food and drink. No longer would I stagger from disaster to disaster, from one lacerating nightmare to another; I'd be the sunlit clearing and the stream where my family would come to drink their fill of the milk of human kindness. And it seemed to me that this final adventure would be even more dangerous than the others, because, for once, I couldn't imagine how it would end.

'It's terrible,' I said, 'but I feel I'll never be able to imagine anyone else but you.'

'No more shall I. That's why we must be very careful, you especially.'

'Are you still thinking about Julius?'

'Yes,' he said gravely. 'He's a man who's only interested in power and possessions. This attitude of disinterestedness he has adopted towards you scares me. I wouldn't be so scared if he made specific demands on you. But I'd rather not talk to you about it; it's not for me to disabuse you. But when that happens, I want to be the one you turn to.'

'To say I told you so?'

'No, to comfort you. It's never much fun having one's eyes opened. You're bound to hate whoever is responsible, and I'd rather it wasn't me.'

All this seemed pretty vague and implausible. In my euphoria, I was more inclined to see Julius as a godfather than a tyrant. So I gave a noncommital smile and got up to go. I had an appointment with Ducreux at six o'clock to choose some covers for the magazine. Louis came with me as far as the door and then went on his way. He was going to have dinner with Didier.

I was a few minutes late and I walked in on tiptoe. In the office next to mine, I could hear Ducreux talking on the telephone and I didn't want to disturb him. The door was open. I sat down at my desk. It was some time before I realized that he was talking about me.

'. . . It puts me in a very delicate position,' Ducreux was saying. 'When you asked me to take her on, I had no good reason to refuse. After all, she needed a job and for financial reasons I was short of staff. And since you offered to pay her yourself . . . No, nothing has changed, except that I assumed she knew the position. For the past two months, ever since you decided – for her sake – to back my magazine, I've observed her carefully, and she knows nothing at all . . . I don't know what your intentions are . . . Yes, of course I realize that it's none of my business, but if she suddenly discovers the truth, it'll make me look rather unscrupulous, which I'm not. It'll look like a deliberate trap . . .'

He stopped talking because I was standing in the doorway looking at him, appalled. He hung up gently, gestured to the chair facing him and I sat down automatically. We went on looking at one another.

'I don't suppose there's anything more I need add,' he said.

He was paler and greyer than ever.

'No,' I said. 'I think I've go it straight now.'

'I saw nothing wrong with what Monsieur Cram suggested, and I honestly thought you knew about it. I began to feel a little worried two months ago, when he asked me to give you more work, to send you abroad . . . Actually, I didn't really understand what was going on until you introduced me to Louis Dalet.'

I could hardly breathe; I was ashamed of myself, of him, of Julius and, above all, I thought bitterly, despairingly, of the image of an intelligent, sensitive, cultivated young woman that I had built up of myself between these crumbling walls.

'It doesn't matter,' I said. 'Of course it was too good to be true.'

'It makes no difference, you know,' Ducreux said. 'I'm quite prepared to ring Monsieur Cram back, renounce the new magazine and keep you on.'

I smiled at him, or rather tried to smile at him but it wasn't easy.

'That would be too stupid,' I said. 'I'm going to have to leave, but I can't believe Julius would be so petty as to take it out on you.'

There was a moment's silence and we looked at one another with a sort of tenderness.

'My offer remains open,' he said, 'and if you ever need a friend . . . I'm sorry, Josée, I took you on as a whim.'

'That's what I am,' I said quietly, 'at least, that's what I used to be. I'll give you a ring.'

Then I hurried out, because my eyes were filling with tears. I glanced round at the shabby desk, the papers, the photographs, the typewriters, at what had been the comforting background to an illusion, and I left. I didn't stop at the first café, where our happy group always congregated, but at the next. Something hardened inside me and I felt obsessed by the need to get at the truth, whatever it might be. It was no good my asking Julius. He would transform this treachery, this buying of me, into nothing more than an act of gallantry, a gift to a distraught young woman. I could think of only one person who hated me enough not to mince words, and that was the ferocious Mme Debout. I telephoned her, and, as luck would have it, she was in.

'I'll be waiting for you,' she said.

She didn't add 'at the ready', but I was sure, as the taxi took me to her, that she would be redoing her face and hair, looking at herself in the mirror with triumphant anticipation.

I was in her drawing room, it was a beautiful evening, and I felt perfectly calm.

'You're not going to tell me that you weren't aware of all that?'

'I'm not going to tell you anything,' I said, 'because you wouldn't believe me.'

'True enough. Do you mean to say you weren't aware that one doesn't find flats in the rue de Bourgogne for 450 francs a month? You weren't aware that couturiers – *my* couturier, by the way – aren't in the habit of dressing unknown young women for nothing? You weren't aware that there are scores of young women much better educated than you who'd give anything for that job on the magazine?'

'I ought to have known, it's true.'

'Julius is a very patient man and this little charade could have gone on indefinitely, whatever amorous escapades you got up to. Julius has never been known to give up. But I can tell you that as far as his friends are concerned, and especially me, it was becoming intolerable to see him at the beck and call of a . . .'

'Of a what?' I said.

'Let's just say, at your beck and call.'

'Fine.'

And I burst out laughing, which disconcerted her some-

136

what. She exuded such a palpable aura of hatred, contempt and incredulity that it made her almost funny.

'And what in your opinion did Julius want?'

'What *does* Julius want, you mean! He told me from the first: he wanted to see that you had an interesting, agreeable life, to give you time to sow a few wild oats which eventually would bring you back to him. Don't imagine you'll escape quite so easily. You haven't seen the last of us yet, my dear Josée.'

'Oh yes, I have,' I said. 'You see, I've decided to live with Louis Dalet and I'm leaving for the country next week.'

'And when you're tired of him, you'll be back, Julius will be there and you'll be only too glad to see him again. Your little dramas amuse him, your bogus innocence makes him laugh, but don't go too far.'

'If I understand you correctly,' I said, 'he also despises me . . .'

'Not really. He says that you're basically decent and that you'll give in to him in the end.'

I stood up, and this time I smiled with no effort at all.

'I don't think so. You see, your contempt has blinded you to such a degree that you've failed to realize that you and your intrigues bore me profoundly. Julius's intrigues hurt me because I'm fond of him, but as for you, really . . .'

The jibe went home. Of all words, 'boredom' was surely the most intolerable, the most devastating to her, and my composure must have been more frightening that any outburst of anger.

'I'll pay Julius and the couturier bit by bit,' I said. 'I'll speak to my ex-mother-in-law personally and we'll soon get this business of my alimony settled, in spite of Julius.'

She stopped me on the doorstep; she looked worried.

'What are you going to tell Julius?'

'Nothing,' I said. 'I shan't see him again.'

Once outside, I strode down the street humming to myself out loud. I was filled with a sort of exultant anger. At last I was done with all the lies, the subterfuges, the enticements. Unwittingly I had been bribed for the amusement of these squalid people. How they must have laughed at my air of independence and my escapades. They had really put it over on me. I was heartbroken, yes, but also relieved: at last I knew where I stood. They had put a pretty gold collar around my neck, and the chain had snapped; it was better that way.

As I was packing my meagre wardrobe, which consisted of the few clothes Alan had left me, I told myself sardonically that self-respect was clearly not my forte. Through a mixture of blindness and optimism, I had allowed Julius to make me look contemptible in the eyes of his friends and no doubt in his too. And this I couldn't forgive him, because if he had really loved me, in spite of his contempt, he shouldn't have allowed others to judge me. I cast a grateful glance around the little flat in which I had gradually cured myself of Alan, in which I had got to know Louis – that illusory but cosy haven. I put the dog on the lead and we walked sedately down the stairs. The landlady, another of Julius's stooges, had the grace not to show herself. I found a small hotel where, lying on the bed with the dog curled at my feet and my suitcase on the floor, I watched the night fall on six months of my life and the death of a friendship.

The summer, radiant and mild, was spent in Louis's house. He had made no comment on my story. He had simply been more loving and attentive than usual. Didier visited us often. The three of us looked for a house on the outskirts of Paris and in the end we found one near Versailles. We were happy, and the kind of moral ache, the fatigue and depression that had accompanied my flight wore off after a month. I hadn't written to Julius, I hadn't replied to his letters, I hadn't even read them. I no longer saw anyone from that little circle; I saw Louis's friends and old friends of mine. I felt I had been saved. Saved from a danger which, because it was vague and impalpable, I now realized was a thousand times worse than any I had encountered before: I had narrowly escaped taking myself too seriously, belonging to people I didn't care about, being profoundly bored and refusing to recognize this boredom for what it was. I was coming back to life – doubly so indeed, since in August I knew that I was expecting Louis's child. We decided to baptize both child and dog together, for the latter was still without a name.

A few days after we moved into our new house, I was crossing the avenue de la Grande-Armée in Paris in the rain when I ran into Julius. A Daimler came out of a side street. I recognized it at once and stopped dead. Julius got out and came towards me. He looked thinner.

'Josée,' he said, 'at last! I knew you'd come back.'

I looked at him, I looked at this stubborn little man. It seemed to me that for the first time I was seeing him face to face. He had the same blue eyes, glittering behind their glasses, the same navy-blue suit, the same inert hands. I had to make an enormous effort to remember that for a long time this man had been for me the very symbol of reassurance. Now he seemed to me a stranger, at once disquieting and dull, a crackpot.

'Are you still angry with me? That's all over, isn't it?'

'Yes, Julius,' I said. 'It's over.'

'I suppose you've realized that it was all for your own good. No doubt I went about things in a rather clumsy way.'

He smiled, clearly delighted with himself. I had the same impression as the first time at the Salina, of being in the presence of an unknown and completely alien mechanism. I couldn't remember the smallest exchange between us; all I could recall was a monologue by the sea, the only time he had shown himself to me in a remotely comprehensible light, and it was the memory of this that made me hesitate instead of running away.

'I've kept in touch with your movements all through the summer,' he added. 'I know the Sologne as well as you do yourself.'

'Those private detectives of yours again . . .'

He grinned.

'You surely didn't imagine that I'd stop keeping an eye on you.'

Suddenly I was overcome with fury and the words were out of my mouth before I had time to think.

'Did your private detectives tell you I was expecting a baby?'

He was momentarily taken aback, then he recovered himself.

'But that's marvellous news, Josée. The child will be very well brought up by us.'

'It's Louis's child,' I said. 'We're getting married next month.'

Then, to my astonishment, to my horror, his face convulsed, his eyes filled with tears and he began literally to stamp his feet on the pavement, waving his arms in the air.

'It's not true!' he shouted, 'it's not true, it can't be true!'

I stared at him, aghast, and suddenly the chauffeur appeared behind him and grasped him by the shoulders just as he was about to hit me.

'That child belongs to me,' Julius screamed, 'and you too, you belong to me!'

'Monsieur Cram,' said the chauffeur, pulling him back, 'Monsieur Cram . . .'

'Leave me alone!' shouted Julius. 'Leave me alone! It's not true, I tell you that child belongs to me!'

The chauffeur dragged him away and I shook myself out of my stupor, turned on my heels and rushed into the nearest café. For a long time I sat there with my teeth chattering, trying to pull myself together. I didn't dare leave: I was afraid I might see Julius still standing there in the same spot, choking and stamping his feet and shedding those terrible tears of fury, disappointment, and perhaps love. I telephoned Didier, who came to pick me up and take me home.

Two months later I heard that Julius A. Cram was dead. He had died, I gathered, of a heart attack due to over-indulgence in pep pills, tranquillizers and other nostrums. Our lives had crossed but remained obstinately parallel, obstinately apart. We had never seen each other except in profile, and we had never loved each other. He had dreamt only of possessing me, I only of escaping from him: that was all, and on reflection it was a rather pathetic story. Nevertheless I knew that once time had effected its usual sorting-out process in my tender memory, all that my mind's eye would retain of him would be that tuft of white hair emerging from a hammock, and that I would simply hear his hesitant and weary voice saying to me, 'because ever since I've known you, I've never been bored'.

More About Penguins and Pelicans

Penguinews , which appears every month, contains
details of all the new books issued by Penguins
as they are published. It is supplemented by our
stocklist, which includes around 5,000 titles.

A specimen copy of *Penguinews* will be sent to you
free on request. Please write to Dept EP, Penguin
Books Ltd, Harmondsworth, Middlesex, for your copy.

In the U.S.A.: For a complete list of books available
from Penguins in the United States write to Dept CS,
Penguin Books, 625 Madison Avenue, New York,
New York 10022.

In Canada: For a complete list of books available from
Penguins in Canada write to Penguin Books Canada Ltd,
2801 John Street, Markham, Ontario L3R 1B4.